Gareth Clarke

THE ENIGMA OF BEING

HZPublishing

Copyright © 2023 by Gareth Clarke

All rights reserved. No part of this book may be reproduced or used in any manner without written permission of the copyright owner except for the use of quotations in a book review. For more information, address: garethclarke137@gmail.com

HZPublishing

The Enigma of Being

The Madwoman in the Attic

Desdemona

The Church

The Decision

Kira

The Girl with the Shopping Bags

The Wedding Invitations

The Implant

The Female Metaphysician

Zombie Parade

When Evening Falls

The Unexpected Rise of Lord Fukkata

The Madwoman in the Attic

I'm kept up in the attic. There's a lift they had installed at great expense (they never grow tired of telling people that) as there was no possibility of extending outwards into a granny annexe. Time to annexe granny. Sounds like something they did in the war. I forget what. Or a growth that needs cutting out. We'll have you in next Tuesday. It's only a benign annexe, we can do that under a local. Of course they don't really want me here at all. Why would they. Why would anyone, come to that. We're just a nuisance at our age. Expendable.

My daughter Joyce took out power of attorney. For my own good apparently, as sometimes I'm absent-minded. So she said to anyone who asked. Though in fact I've still got all my marbles. I can still do the crosswords when my eyes aren't too bad, the ones in the Mirror anyway. Anyhow, turns out she did it for her own good as well. Cleaned out my account over the course of six months. Spent the lot. I wondered at the time where they found the money for the extension and the patio and the new car and the three weeks holiday in Peru. I wasn't invited, of course. I'd just be an encumbrance, cramp their style. Turns out I was paying for their style. It was more my style than theirs. That was when I lived just around the corner. She'd come to visit once a fortnight for about ten minutes. Just to shout at me about something, crash a few things around then go again, slamming the door behind her. I used to cry for a bit after. But then you get used to it. You can get used to almost anything just so long as you're not expecting anything better.

One time when I was still living near Joyce I took my other daughter Helen and her family out for dinner and my card wouldn't go through. I didn't know what was going on. It's contactless, but when that didn't work I tried putting my PIN in instead. Card not accepted. Turns out there wasn't enough left in the account. Joyce had cleaned it out bar a few coppers. Helen ended up paying for everything. So that was the end of my largesse. And my nest-egg. So much for leaving a little legacy for the kiddies. Joyce and Helen had a nasty set to and have never spoken since. I wish now I'd never said anything.

I had some tests at the hospital last week, scans, for the headaches I've been getting. Found nothing. Ha no surprise there, I said, but they didn't get it. Different culture, humour doesn't always travel. Always pleasant though. At least they never get impatient with me when I'm a bit slow, unlike some who think they're hiding it but aren't. I think the headaches might be something to do with my eyesight, straining to read things. I used to read all the time, but it's such a nuisance now I tend to stick to the telly.

In fact it's become a whole production just getting up out of my chair. Shuffling forward, then trying to push myself up. You get so stiff, that's the thing. When you're young you think it'll never happen to you, but truth is it creeps up on you. Sometimes when I do manage to get up I almost fall over trying to get my balance, just trying to get my legs to work. And you never don't feel tired, even after doing nothing. I do a few jobs around the place and I'm done in. But they say it's ungrateful to complain. Not that I've got anyone to complain to. They say you're lucky to have reached your age. I don't feel lucky. But apparently I'm lucky to be eighty-one and stuck up here with no-one to talk to. To be fair I've got my own room with a kitchenette and an en-suite so that is lucky compared to some. So there you go. My good fortune.

Of course they never leave me alone with the kids. They say it'd be too much for me but we all know the real reason. They must think I'm daft if they think I don't twig. They're Christians, evangelists of all things. Never in a million years thought a daughter of mine'd be one of them. But she got it off him, her husband Neville. You don't meet many Nevilles these days. Probably for the best. They don't want me here but they're feathering their nest in the afterlife and saving their souls by doing the Christian thing by me. I never believed in any of that stuff personally. Never willingly went to church, never said any prayers, just mumbled nonsense to myself if I was ever dragged there. I always thought I might just as well be talking to myself - which I do, by the way. Anyway at least they're not feathering their nest with my money, so that's something.

So I'm down to my pension now. I try to make sure I spend it all as soon as it comes into the account apart from a few quid for contingencies. I pay them rent and something for the heating. They said it wasn't necessary, but I'd feel doubly uncomfortable if I didn't. And I get a fortnightly delivery from Tesco. Mainly just things I can microwave. And apart from a few little gifts for the kiddies (which are always vetted) if there's anything left I give it to charity, animals mainly. As if I care about any of it. I couldn't care less.

I'm only allowed down at certain times. They control the lift. I'm not allowed, they say it'd be too dangerous, I might get stuck. I don't see how. It's like being some animal at the zoo. Feeding time. Throw the monkey a banana. But don't get too close. I often think of Frank when I'm sitting up in my enclosure feeling lucky. He was a good husband, always supported me and doted on his girls. If he could have seen how they turned out after he was gone. Oh they're alright really, both of them. They're no worse than many, even Joyce. The temptation was there, so she fell into it. Give us this day our daily bread, and forgive us our trespasses as we forgive those who trespass against us, and lead us not into temptation, but deliver us from evil. Amen. I still remember that. I could recite the whole thing. So why didn't God deliver

Joyce from temptation, that's what I want to know. Make himself useful for once. I blame it on God. At least I would if there was one. Anyway I've forgiven her. It's all water under the bridge.

I wish they'd learn to forgive, though. It's been seven years now since Frank died and they still haven't forgiven me. Seven years, hard to believe it's been that long. We married in 1962. That winter was proper cold, year of the big freeze. We used to spend a lot of the time in bed, young love and all that. You never get winters like that now. It's funny to have lived long enough to notice changes like that. I was twenty-two, Frank a couple of years older. It was just before the Beatles and the Swinging Sixties and miniskirts and all that. I used to dress like it was still 1950. You'd never catch me in a miniskirt or hotpants. Now I think I should have given them a go while I still had the looks. And the legs. The legs aren't up to much these days, no miniskirt for me. Now there's an image to conjure with.

I was bonny back then though. I sometimes look back through photos from those years, early sixties. We made a good-looking couple. I sometimes wore my hair shortish, not quite a pixie cut, but heading in that direction. That was my concession. Pretty face, slim, good legs. And Frank was a lovely looking bloke. There he is, tall, with his hair as dark as could be and swept back, piled up on his head all shiny like they did then before the long hair started. Smiling. Always smiling in the photos. Holding Joyce or Helen when they came along, proud as punch. You never know what's in store for you. Just as well.

We put off having kids for a long time, unusual for those days, partly at least because I had a career, which was also unusual for a woman back then. I'd a first degree and a masters in chemistry - well I've still got them, I suppose. I was the only girl in the department, and there weren't many in the university as a whole. And coming from an all-girls grammar school that was a bit of a shock. Then I worked as a lab technician and research assistant for several different companies which I thoroughly enjoyed. I was in no hurry to have kids - I think Frank was more keen than I was - but anyway he was happy for us to wait and he supported me being at work which most men back then wouldn't have. Funnily enough Helen did the same, waited till her mid-thirties, though of course it's much more the norm these days. Anyway I quit work when I was thirty-six and pregnant with Helen. It was a wrench especially as I had the chance of doing some interesting research, but I'd had a good run and you couldn't combine having babies with a career like you can these days.

Neither of us knew anything about motor neurone disease beyond the name. We had no idea when Frank got the first signs of weakness in his right arm and found it difficult suddenly to pick up his cup of tea that it was a death sentence. Eighteen months. That's all it took for him to be permanently confined to a wheelchair and completely dependent for everything. The only compensation, if you can call it that, is that he could still just about take food and drink by mouth with me feeding him, so he didn't need a feeding tube. But over time his breathing became worse and worse, which meant repeated trips to hospital. It reduces all your functions bit by bit, though Frank's mind was clear as a bell to the end. But there can be step changes. You can wake up one day and find yourself that much worse or unable to do something you could do the day before. That's what happened with Frank anyway. After a bad bout of pneumonia which required a hospital stay he suddenly needed a ventilator to help his overnight breathing. That was the final straw. That and the pain. Towards the end he was in constant pain. But it wasn't just the physical suffering, it's the loss of dignity. I was in my seventies and I did what I could, but we still needed a team of carers for all the heavy work and to help with the intimate stuff, cleaning up and so on.

He always called me Babs. It was just the way he was, always affectionate. He'd call me Barbara only when it was something really serious. Towards the end it wasn't easy for him to say anything, and I was about the only one who could understand him. One day he said, 'I've had enough Barbara. I just can't take any more of this.' He was in tears, I was in tears. Seeing him like that nearly broke my heart. A big strapping man like Frank reduced to that. But I had to stay strong for him. He'd finally reached the end of what he could endure, but beyond the point where he could do anything about it himself. The thing he feared most was his breathing getting even worse and his lungs getting so congested that in the end you choke or suffocate, drown in your own mucus and saliva. So he knew exactly what he wanted and what he wanted me to do. Of course any kind of help to end someone's life is against the law and Frank was worried for me on that score, but I was determined to do whatever it took. We couldn't afford to go to Switzerland. At least we could have, but Frank insisted he didn't want all that money spent on himself. As if he was thinking of buying himself a sports car. I wish he had done now. I wish now he'd spent it all on himself.

They said later they hadn't had the chance to say goodbye. They had every opportunity. Not right at the end, maybe, but before that. They knew how ill he was and how much pain he was in. They knew he couldn't take it anymore. They could have said anything they wanted before the very end. Anyway we always kept things private. That's just the way we preferred it. They'd never have let us do what we knew had to be done if they'd known. So it had to be like that. The mistake I made was being honest and upfront after with the GP. I didn't want there to be any lies. Anyway they might have been able to tell from the autopsy.

I'd prepared a cocktail of painkillers and sleeping pills I'd put to one side over the previous couple of months. He could only swallow with difficulty by then, but we managed somehow. He became drowsy, then fell unconscious. Then after telling him one last time how much I loved him I got a pillow, put it over his face and pressed down. I hadn't intended to do it, but I suddenly felt I didn't want him to die alone. Sounds daft saying it like that, I could've just held his hand. But I owed it to Frank to make sure his suffering was truly over. And so there we were, still a couple, pressed together, even in death. There's no way of properly explaining it. So I stayed like that, pressing down on his face, my tears making a wet patch on the pillow, for probably five minutes. Then I got up, put the pillow to one side and looked down at him. All the pain had gone out of his face. He looked almost happy for the first time in a long time.

When I told the GP what I'd done she called the police. They were quite nasty about it, quite aggressive. Said they were going to throw the book at me, make an example of me. I was treated like a criminal, put in a cell for thirty six hours. Forced to use the toilet in the cell as they wouldn't let me use proper facilities. The solicitor said it would be best if we told the court the balance of my mind was disturbed at the time, and it's true I was depressed and to a degree suicidal after. On top of everything I had to endure my daughters' anger at what we'd done, the recriminations. There were many times I wished I'd taken the same cocktail as Frank. But I knew I had to stay alert to make sure he passed without suffering any further. I spent a couple of weeks in a psychiatric unit. The GP, same one that called the police, thought I might do something to myself, but though I'd thought about it at the time, afterwards I hadn't the nerve. Later on the charge was reduced from murder to aiding and abetting a suicide, and I got a suspended sentence. The judge called it a tragic case.

The madwoman in the attic. Apparently it's a family joke. I heard it from their youngest, Richard. He's only four, didn't know what he was saying, though his speech is very clear for his age. They tried to shush him but it was too late. At least they had the grace to look embarrassed. So after that I thought, well, if I'm just a joke I'll play up to it and pretend to be worse than I am. You know, play the eccentric old woman. Just now and again, and nothing much, just something to make them think twice and make them think they've got good reason for leaving me stuck up here ninety percent of the time. Not very sensible, but sometimes you need to push back a bit for the sake of your sanity. I'm not eccentric at all really, I'm down to earth. Just a normal woman trying to make the best of things. I wish Frank was still here though. Always so kind and easy-going, but he wouldn't have stood for any of this nonsense. But that's it, I'm on my own now. Nobody to turn to. The madwoman. I cry myself to sleep sometimes. It's no life.

Desdemona

Truth is I'm not that desperately keen on human beings. Who is, you say. In fact for the most part I absolutely hate the fuckers. I'm just being honest. I find other people generally speaking intensely annoying. I don't think I've always thought that way. It's probably working in hospitality, too much close contact. So I take a real pleasure in killing people in games. But as for Lisa, my now and forever ex-girlfriend, I don't hate her, even now, despite everything. I couldn't say for sure I ever really loved her either - or even liked her that much - certainly not that crazy out-of-body feeling where they take over your mind, night and day. But I certainly never hated her - or blamed her. It was all my own doing. Yet Desdemona was different in every way, and she was able to unerringly capture me emotionally right from the get-go.

*

How it began. Before starting *Fallout* yet again I'd been playing *GreedFall*. It's fun to play and beautifully designed, with atmospheric settings, and interesting characters and concept. There's flaws of course - the NPCs do next to nothing, the combat is not that great, and the interiors are generic, the layout and detailing repetitive. And the game's got plenty of glitches, but I don't particularly mind that, in fact I quite enjoy it so long as it doesn't screw up the gameplay which it doesn't to any great extent. *Skyrim* has loads of glitches - Bethesda's famous for it - but it's still one of the greatest games of all time. And *Oblivion*, which is consciously hilarious, but just manages to walk the line between entertainment and self-parody. I had been planning to play *Deus Ex: Mankind Divided,* which I'd just got (for some reason I didn't get it when it first came out). It looked amazing in the trailers, and lived up to it (with minor reservations) when I did get around to playing it, and strangely enough there were clear parallels in the game with Desdemona's core beliefs.

*

So anyway I'd started *Fallout 4* for something like the sixth or seventh time. Not always to finish it, but just to give it a go and say hello once more to the game and the characters. I find it relaxing. So I thought I might as well play it again at least part of the way through even though like I said I'd just got a new game I could have played instead. Truth is I just couldn't summon up the mental energy at that particular point. Being stuck inside all the time - apart from going for a run once a day - is not all it's cracked up to be.

And then I always get sucked in when I watch the start. I think partly it's the look on the face of that poor cretinous bastard who despite the storyline obviously couldn't give a shit about his wife and child. Whatever face shape or look or style you decide on you can tell there's nothing at all going on behind his eyes. I always give the poor fuck zero on charisma and intelligence, and maximum on luck, because he surely needs it.

*

Another reason I like the game so much is that I've always been attracted to the idea of catastrophe and apocalypse and general devastation. I just love the idea of everything breaking down and turning to shit. Don't ask me why, I've just always thought it would be a huge improvement to have a clear out. Then make a fresh start when life begins to return. It'd be like a reset. There's no way back from the fucking mess everything's in now, that's for sure. So it seems like a pretty good plan to me. Just to get rid of all the lunatics. Not that there's not a high probability that they'd just be replaced by other lunatics. But on the other hand there's that small chance that things might turn out better next time around.

*

So I'd been wandering around in the game for a couple of hours. And then I watched some crap on TikTok. Twenty minutes is my limit where those brain-dead exhibitionists are concerned. And after that I watched this couple on YouTube climb an abandoned chimney over 300m tall, supposedly the highest chimney in

Europe. They'd climbed up this thing and there they were at the top casually walking around the rim, one slip or gust of wind away from death. Silly bastards. I was really hoping one of them would slip and fall, preferably inside the chimney and pull the other one in with them. But then they sat together on the rim as if they were in the countryside somewhere having a picnic. When that finished I watched some trucks getting stuck in mud for a while or washed away by a swollen river and then some heavy machinery, cranes and diggers and suchlike falling over.

*

Liam and Lisa. Lisa and Liam. I always found that faintly ridiculous. With those names we should have had matching jumpers. Imagine if we'd ever got married. Lisa and Liam request the pleasure of your company on their special day. Together with their families Lisa and Liam joyfully invite you to their wedding celebration. The honour of your presence is requested for the wedding of Lisa and Liam as we celebrate their union in marriage. We're getting hitched - come if you want, don't if you don't, we really don't give a shit. Oh the B and G? Didn't I mention? It's Lisa and Liam. Not much chance of that now.

*

The first time I met Lisa's parents - Geoff and Mary, would you believe - another hideous combination - was totally gruesome. In fact it never improved much above the gruesome (with more than a hint of the bizarre), but the first time's always the worst because you're nervous, and though you've got no expectations you hope for the best. After that you know the score much better so it's not a shock and you're better prepared. Lisa's old man was just a cipher. Nice enough, quiet, an excellent climber. But the mother, Mary, was the one with the balls in that relationship. Or a screw loose. Probably both. A genuinely strange, harsh woman, possibly insane. And you can't help wondering how much of that must rub off. Still, who could not love Lisa. And why. Answers on a postcard. The first hundred correct answers win a prize: a date with Lisa.

*

I was supposed to make myself useful during lockdown. Not knowing if I'd even have a job after it was all over. At the time wondering how long it would take for things to get back to normal, if ever. There's zero job security in hospitality at the best of times. Not that I was too bothered, to be honest. I needed a change of direction after doing the same mindless routines at several different hotels for the past three years since leaving uni with a degree in English Literature, described in the prospectus as having 'universal appeal to employers as proof of key transferable skills, the development of analytic, linguistic and creative abilities, unique literary and critical faculties' and so on and so on and so forth. Which no doubt was why I ended up in hospitality. By the way I should perhaps make it clear that there was never any intention of actually cheating on Lisa. It was all just a game, just something to pass the time.

*

She'd been on a late shift. I'd been out earlier and got some stuff in. Something for her to microwave when she got in. I'd made something for myself and ate it watching a compilation of people falling over. Bored out of my mind at this point. Bone-deep boredom. I felt a sudden extreme urge to do something, anything, just to create some excitement and try to avoid going completely nuts. And I'm kind of thinking like fuck lockdown. Everyone's sick to their dick of it now, and in any case we're only locked down because of the senile and superannuated. Not to mention that if Lisa got it she was guaranteed to pass it on to me. Anyway like I say it was mainly all the old fuckers dying of it, and as they'd completely screwed the young over Brexit, so far as I was concerned it's like, Karma, man.

*

After greeting each other, before taking a shower she'd go through to the kitchen and look pointedly at the cooker and oven or the sink, especially if there happened to be a few dirty plates there, but say nothing. Another thing, I never mentioned it so I guess she wasn't aware of it, but her uniform always stank when she came in off a shift. I don't know what it is about working on the wards. Smelled like chemicals and sweat and shit all mixed together. Still, at least she always put the uniform straight in the washer and took a shower. So that was something.

*

I'd already had the idea of trying to write a story during lockdown - maybe even a full-length novel, a long-held ambition. The difficult question as ever was what to actually write about. I could never seem to think of anything but the eternal tedious lockdown, people incarcerated within their homes, bickering, growing their hair, taking drugs, getting pissed, screaming at each other and generally going insane and building a raft of resentments in their heads. Of course the other thing they might do is go on the internet and watch porn, or listen to music or play games or whatever. Even after another round of deliberation and another shot or several of Jack Daniels I was getting absolutely nowhere.

*

Then came my great idea: what about someone so bored out of their tits with being stuck inside doing nothing and seeing nobody that they join an online dating site, just for a laugh and to chat people up. But then something happens. I wasn't sure what - I hadn't really worked out any details at this point. It was just a vague concept - somebody playing some kind of trivial game - but the idea did seem to have potential.

And then I thought - why not play a little game of my own as research for this would-be novel, and just to up the ante. To digress for a moment and open the window a fraction on a harmless kink. I've always had a thing for older women. Nothing wrong with that, you might say. In fact I've always had this fantasy of being seduced by a woman of a certain age, maybe late fifties, early sixties. I think it's that knowingness or deadness in the eyes. The look that says they've seen and done everything sexually. And also the thought that hopefully there were no depths to which at some time or other they hadn't sunk. And might well be prepared to sink again, given the opportunity. That combination, the possibility that they may be desperate, so therefore up for anything, coupled with all the perverted tricks they've surely picked up over the years.

*

So I joined this well-known free online dating site whose name I won't promote, not being paid to do so. As I was saying, I wanted for not necessarily the purest of motives to chat to older women. The problem being that on this site you can only message people a maximum of fourteen years older or younger than your stated age. Which didn't really work for me. And so came my second inspiration. Which was to be somebody else entirely. Somebody much older - say early sixties, with kids, long marriage, divorced a while ago.

At first I was thinking photos would be a problem, but then I remembered my uncle, a friendly, good-looking guy with a kind of Paul Hollywood vibe who'd died three years earlier in his early sixties of a heart attack. I asked my mum (shielding due to asthma) to send me a few photos of Uncle Eric, which she did. I just said I didn't have any and I'd forgotten what he looked like. Mum seemed pleased I'd thought about him. So now that I had some pics, next I had to invent a profile. And in trying to discover who I was, I tested out a few possible options.

*

LR888
Asking for a friend
62 year old man, 6' 0" (183cm)

INTERESTED IN CASUAL DATING

BASICS
- Writer
- Divorced, I want to date but nothing serious, Seeking a woman, Dating
- High school
- Cockborough, England

LIFESTYLE
- Doesn't Smoke
- Drinks Socially
- Doesn't Do Drugs
- Is Non-Religious
- All Kids are Over 18

BIO
- 6' 0" (183cm)
- Brown
- Aries
- Average body type
- Brown

ABOUT LR888

Regrets, I have a few, But then again, too many to mention. I did what I should never have had to do, And saw it through without redemption. I've lived (if you can call it that), I've travelled each and every B-road, but more, much less than this, I did it somebody else's way. For what is a person, what has he or she got, if not him or herself, then he or she has naught, To say the words he or she truly feels, and not the words of someone called Neil, The record shows, I took the blows, and did it somebody else's way. Yes, the record shows, I took the blows - and did it somebody else's - WAAAAAAAAAAY.

INTERESTS
- football
- snooker
- tv

- reading
- walking
- football
- writing
- but not football
- darts
- comedy

or alternatively,

LR888
Now that's interesting!
59 year old man, 6' 0" (183cm)

ABOUT LR888
I like travelling, or not travelling, conversation, or silence, buildings, or open spaces, blue skies, or not, floor coverings, or stained floorboards, seagulls, or not, vanilla ice cream, or not, MotoGP, or not, Chris Eubank, or not, Chris Evert, or not, Christingle (or not).

p.s. I accidentally gave the wrong DOB. I'm actually 102. But hair dye, plenty of exercise, overdosing on vitamin E and abstaining from smoking, alcohol, sex or any other form of pleasure keeps me looking relatively young.

INTERESTS
- travelling
- conversation
- buildings

- blue skies
- floor coverings
- seagulls
- vanilla ice cream
- MotoGP
- Chris Eubank
- Chris Evert
- Christingle

or maybe,

LR888
Shallow non-spiritual vegetarian seeks similar
61 year old man, 6' 0" (183cm)

ABOUT LR888
Hi, I'm reliable, hard wearing and durable. Guaranteed for a minimum of ten years under normal operating conditions or your money back. Many advantages over comparable products. Safe, economical, built to the highest standards as approved by industry experts. Rated highly in all customer satisfaction surveys. Long-lasting, built-in comfort. Highest mileage ever obtained in exhaustive testing. Handsome, buttressed side walls, wider, flatter tread giving more traction, more wear. Be the envy of your friends and neighbours! Don't hesitate, change your life! Buy now!

or maybe even,

LR888
Well, hello there. My, it's been a long, long time.
63 year old man, 6' 0" (183cm)

ABOUT LR888
Hi, thank you for reading my profile. If you've got this far, congratulations! You win a non-existent prize. So what to say. There are so many things one could say, and so many potential starting points. One feels one is almost overwhelmed by all the potential ways of going about this, and all the many things one could say. But one must say something. So one thinks that what one has decided is that the most important thing one could say is this. Thank you very much.

*

Having amused myself with a few potential profiles, it was time to get down to business and think seriously about character, just as if I was trying to invent a character in a novel. To make the strongest possible distinction between 'him' and me (and for my own entertainment), I decided to make him the direct opposite of me in as many ways as I could. So I came up with a highly spiritual vegan feminist, an elderly right-on left-leaning woolly-minded pacifist. And that's what I decided to run with. Which wasn't an altogether great idea as it turned out, as the vegan feminist thing is a 24-carat solid gold turn-off for most women.

But anyway I forgot about it more or less straight away and thereafter continually wandered off message. I could always have changed it, but once I got chatting to Desdemona and given she'd presumably read my profile I was pretty much stuck with it. Anyway she didn't seem to pick up that much or indeed at all on discrepancies. I think she was too focused on herself and her own message to do more than occasionally point out something that didn't add up, or that made her eyebrows waggle, as she would say.

*

DESDEMONA
I'm shaking my head, getting sawdust all over
57 year old female, 5' 8" (172cm)

INTERESTED IN CASUAL DATING

BASICS
- None of your beeswax
- High school
- Divorced
- North East

LIFESTYLE
- Doesn't Smoke
- Doesn't Do Drugs
- Doesn't Have Kids
- Drinks Socially

- Is Other Religion
- Does not want children

BIO
- 5' 8" (172cm)
- Caucasian
- Average body type
- Libra
- Mixed Colour

ABOUT DESDEMONA
- IMPORTANT NOTICE!! Just here for the chat, nothing more
- Read the above and take note!
- Humour is a big part of who I am...I love to laugh at the absurdities of life
- Not 'politically correct'
- This place is crammed full with new-agers and pagans and 'humanists'. I'm none of those things....btw

*

April 2020

11.09 PM
L *Hi how are you doing? So what does not politically correct actually mean for you?*

11:27 PM

D *It means that I perhaps have some opinions that are discouraged by the powers that be. I don't enjoy being told what I should think, how I should feel and what I can say. It's gotten out of hand now and what they are really saying is 'You can say what you wish to so long as it tallies with what WE think'. No such thing as freedom of speech anymore and well...they may as well muzzle everyone at birth, then...if we can only say what they allow us to say! Arms folded.*

11:35 PM

L *So what are these opinions that you feel would draw the disapproval of our rulers?*

11:47 PM

L *I've just realised that as a humanist I fall into a category you obviously disdain.*

11:59 PM

D *I did not say that I have disdain for humanists at all. I just wanted to make it clear that I was not in any of the 3 camps I mentioned. You were putting words in my mouth there...not something I relish, I have to say!*

12:03 AM

L *I thought your tone implied it.*

12:19 AM
L *I'm a humanist in that I believe in a rational, evidence-based approach to life, as opposed to the spiritual or religious, as the only logical route to progress and peaceful co-existence.*

12:42 AM
D *I'm not keen that humanists think there is no higher power, no creator and that therefore they are answerable only to themselves for what they do and the lives they lead. To imagine that us flawed human beings can govern our own lives with any great level of success is troubling to me. We are all flawed and therefore are not qualified to know what is ultimately best for ourselves...and we therefore do need guidance on how to manage this thing called living from a Being infinitely more wise than we are. But obviously not believing there is a power greater than Man's you will not therefore agree.*

12:49 AM
L *I just don't see the evidence for any omniscient guiding power in the universe. I reckon we're on our own, however scary that prospect may be. So we have to put faith in ourselves to solve the problems that confront us. Putting your faith and ceding your autonomy to some real or imagined higher authority is a very dangerous thing to do.*

1:02 AM
D *Look at the world around you today. Not much success that I can see in Man managing his own affairs.*

1:22 AM
D *I think the main problem is that intelligence has overtaken more important things. Technological advances have far exceeded the emotional growth of humanity and so technology in my view is not so great a thing. It could be and it should be a great positive but it is not. Too many people addicted to it all at the expense of more rewarding and personally enriching things.*

*

That was my first contact with Desdemona, and already her individuality and eccentricity were coming through loud and clear. And I was already drawn to her, however ludicrous I might think her opinions and 'ideas'. Of course this interaction wasn't and had no prospect of being face to face. She was clear on that from the start. It's there in her profile - Just here for the chat.

Clear in all her opinions, to be fair - clear, wide-eyed, intransigent, implacable - yet with a childlike naive belief in the absolute division of right and wrong, of black and white, of the unalterable truth of her own opinions which I (at one point) found endearing, and more than somewhat lovable - even when she was talking complete and utter bollocks with great conviction while high-handedly patronizing me for failing to grasp the momentous concept which she had in fact merely obliquely hinted at, evasively or occasionally irritably declining to explain or elucidate.

*

I began to call her D after she'd refused to tell me her real name, and after she'd jokingly suggested the name Desdemona. To be honest she didn't seem to care very much one way or the other, prompting me to question why she refused to tell me in the first place. She could even have made something up and I wouldn't have known the difference.

From time to time she put up photos to her profile, after pointlessly refusing to do so when I asked her to. In the first one she's lying in bed looking at the camera. From the brief glimpse of her shoulders, with no sign of t-shirt or nightdress, I guessed that she was naked under the covers. Perhaps giving herself a cheap thrill, knowing that guys would click on her profile and look at the photo. Or of course giving herself a thrill some other way. A composed expression, wide full lips, handsome features, big blue eyes. Even though she's in bed her eyelashes are painted and she's wearing lipstick, a restrained shade of pink accentuating the severe, almost cruel cast of her lips. You wouldn't necessarily deduce from this image the existence of the great sense of humour claimed in her profile. Nor would our interactions provide more than an occasional glimpse, to begin with at least. And another photo presumably taken at the same time, a close-up, staring at the sky, or rather ceiling, with an inscrutable expression.

*

Later, unknown to me - she could never just volunteer anything or accede to any reasonable request without protesting endlessly, and then refusing - she put up a couple more photos from when she was younger. And I'm Oh my fucking Jesus she is (or rather was) simply gorgeous, stunning, quite possibly the sexiest creature that has ever existed. In one she's wearing a black dress with thin straps, looking away from the camera, smiling. A picture on the wall behind her, hair up but with thin wisps coming down either side of her head.

In the other the hair's a completely different colour, a golden orangey blonde, and longer, fuller. The back of her head and top of her shoulders are reflected in the mirror behind her. She's smiling once more, looking almost directly at the camera, the same lustful lips, the same devastating attractiveness. And those eyes, blue like the sky, big and round and altogether astonishing, the pupil a tiny distinct black pinprick in the blue. That picture alone undoes me. And to think of all the strange illogical ridiculous thoughts swirling passionately behind that exquisite façade as she smiles serenely. And of the mystery of who she really was. And of my infatuation.

*

8:35 AM
D   Technology without wisdom and foresight is a dangerous thing....the scientists of today have a God complex and want to change things that should never have been changed.....growing an ear on a mouse's back, cloning creatures, keeping people artificially alive long after their natural life span...changing the genetic make-up of plants and all manner of things that are just off the chart wrong and should never have been done. They nuked the skies for years straight all in the name of 'science and discovery'. They didn't ask us if we minded if they messed things up big time....we live on the planet, too! These people are insane....unfortunately the lunatics really have taken over as far as I can see..

8:58 AM
L   The answer is education. The human race is desperately under-educated, and therefore unable to make informed decisions, participate positively in the democratic process (where there is one), or hold accountable those who should be held accountable for their actions. You only have to look at the USA, where there's a definite possibility that the orange cloth head may be reelected in November.

9:38 AM
D   I don't know much about Trump at all......all I know about him is that his views are controversial. I've been

looking more at the big picture....not so much politicians. I don't believe politicians have any real power....I think they are merely the nodding dogs of the ones who are really in control. Democratic process? Hmm...nice 'concept'.

9:42 AM
L So who really is in control? You're not a disciple of David Icke, by any chance, are you?

9:49 AM
D It's called the 'octopus' in some circles........I'll give you a quote that was said by someone high up in politics about 100 years ago....

Quote by Woodrow Wilson:
"Since I entered politics, I have chiefly had men's views confided to me privately. Some of the biggest men in the United States, in the field of commerce and manufacture, are afraid of something. They know that there is a power somewhere so organised... so subtle... so watchful... so interlocked... so complete... so pervasive.....that they better not speak above their breath when they speak in condemnation of it."

9:59 AM
L Ah, men. You've really got to look out for these so-called men. Of course there's deals and conspiracies

behind closed doors, probably forever. And of course there's much that goes on that we don't know about. But we should be careful not to get too carried away with theories of coherent conspiracies. The Nazis were very hot on conspiracy theories - esp the one where they rolled Bolshevism, Zionism, world finance and World Jewry into one giant conspiracy that controlled the world. Turns out it didn't, but enough people fell for it to create mayhem. So I think we should be wary of following David Icke (you didn't answer my question, by the way - or maybe you did) too far down the garden path. Or we'll find ourselves in the realm of the Matrix, interdimensional beings, shapeshifting lizards, hollow moons etc. etc. etc.

10:26 AM
D I don't think you can have read his quote carefully enough. If you did then you would not have missed the import of his words.

You have made light of his words when what he was actually saying was of great importance and of far reaching consequences.

You might have to (in your words) be careful not to get too 'carried away'.....I'll make my own judgement on that score. I have done the research and when I speak of these things I'm not talking off the top of my head and I don't *take my information from only one source. I'm not a teenager who says things for effect or on a whim...*

As for not answering your question....I only ever answer the questions I wish to....and I allow other people the same right to say 'Next question, please!'.

That last bit...it was amusing to me that where you meant 'you' you put 'we'.....to make it sound less accusatory or dismissive by including yourself in such 'folly'? I'm no stranger to psychology and the tricks used by the Spin Doctors and the 'Perception Management' specialists : -)

10:38 AM
L *Okay, as I'm clearly a bit dim, and have missed the import of the words you quoted, perhaps you would explain to me, clearly and directly, what they mean?*

Of course you don't have to answer any question I put. But if you choose to speak in riddles and evade a straight question, I have little choice but to draw my own conclusions.

As to your last comment, I think you credit me with greater skills than I possess, though I was duly flattered. And btw I intended to be entirely dismissive.

10:53 AM

D *Woodrow Wilson said it perfectly, though he did understate it somewhat in its 'effect'. You do not need me to rephrase it for you.*

And... yes I'm more than comfortable 'evading' a straight question...though, of course, I don't think of it as evading....I think of it more as my not being under any obligation in the first place! I am not answerable to you!

You are perfectly at liberty to draw whatever conclusions you choose. What you believe about me has no bearing on who I am. btw

11:01 AM

L *You ought to be a politician. Within ten minutes you'd have Paxman sweating and twitching in his chair. You're very resourceful. I admire you. In fact I like you, even though you could be said to be just a tad on the spiky side. I think that life with you would be thoroughly entertaining. Shall we go to bed now? I don't even understand your question, and I'm not at all sure you do either. I just said, Shall we - I heard what you said. Do you even know what you mean by bed? Yes, of course, it's something that you - I don't mean bed in that sense. Are you really unaware of the pervasive and subtle hegemony implied by the use of the term? I - You see a physical object without even considering the import or consequences of a term you bandy about with such unthinking abandon. I -You have no concept of the illusion of a bed in this physical reality that does not in fact exist, the unseen forces that plague the very idea of the bed as you understand it. I -*

11:42 AM
D I'm not really spiky all that much...it's just I happened to read a particular book when I was 20 and it had a profound effect on me.....so much so that I don't let anyone push my buttons. That's what it was about.....how not to let people control you, wind you up and so on. How to take control of one's own emotions and not be blown hither and thither by those who would like to control you or have you 'feel' a certain way.

And bed....is simply a wonderful thing we are lucky enough to know these days... heaven on earth....as opposed to a straw palliasse.

*

I had plenty of opportunity when Lisa was on an early or late of chatting to Desdemona for hours at a time. She kept her distance to begin with. Maybe partly because I was not over-friendly at the start as I couldn't be arsed with all the stuff she came out with and supposedly 'believed'. So it took a while for things to take off and for her to reveal her wilder side. And only then did I realise just how much she fancied me/him as my character appeared to her in the image of my dead uncle. I would look at my/his profile photos and try to imagine myself as this attractive white-bearded middle aged/elderly guy. Though it's near impossible to put yourself inside the mind of someone that age. What would I know of sixty? What do they even think about? What is there to think about when you reach that age? You have no future to speak of; it must feel completely pointless. How would somebody of that age even speak? It's just not possible to think like that or put yourself in their place or imagine how the world might look to them. Oh, and the punchline to all of this, is that I never wrote a word of this would-be novel. I was always far too busy chatting with Desdemona.

*

Lisa was pretty, no question about it. Medium height, slim, a kind of ethereal quality that particularly appealed to me at the time. Shoulder-length light-coloured almost blonde hair. Really very pretty when she smiled. We still fucked at that point. Lisa, Lisa. What a darling you were. In her nurse's uniform she looked so inert, almost sterile, the very archetype of the emotionally detached professional carer. To be in her capable hands and wholly dependent on her ministrations makes me fervently hope I never find myself in that precarious position. Not that I would want to touch her or be touched by her in any other setting or situation, you understand. I'm speaking purely hypothetically. Which (I'm starting to believe) in an uncertain world is the only legitimate way to express oneself.

*

I couldn't seem to stop myself from committing small cruelties towards Lisa, with occasional intermissions of emotion and feelings of something that at least felt like love. It was only after we'd rather abruptly and with complete finality parted that I began to realise that these outbursts of impatience and unkindness and even occasional anger were the only way I could think of to disturb and break through that façade of tranquil complacency, at once annoying and false - the lack of any true emotion at any time, merely a tedious, level, empty presentation of pleasantness.

*

In my third year at uni I chose as my main project to create the basic structure and premises and some sample dialogue of a role play game. I developed a special agent/spy type character in the mould of James Bond/Modesty Blaise/Richard Hannay/Dick Tracy etc. I called him Dick Todger, Special Agent. I remember that my module tutor was unamused and in fact particularly po-faced at my choice of name. Which begs the question, why does nobody have a sense of humour anymore. Unless it's standup - which I despise as a very blunt instrument - and which as a general rule tends to focus heavily on the bodily functions, in which case the audience will bray like donkeys. Anyway that's all by the by. Uni is where I met Lisa, that's the point.

I'm not even sure what she was doing there as we didn't attend the same uni. But there I was at a students' union disco with a couple of mates, all hoping to pull, when a tallish girl with long shiny blonde hair, jigging vapidly with a girlfriend, caught my eye. After half a minute or so she happened to turn as she was dancing so that we ended up directly facing each other, maybe a couple of feet apart. After the obligatory mutual once-over, Lisa (for it was she) favoured me with what seemed for all the world like a sincere smile. We managed to exchange a few words over the music, and duly swapped phone numbers. I didn't call her immediately, attracted to her though I was, as I had one or two other hot prospects in mind and wasn't sure at that point which way to go.

A week later I was making my way along a narrow corridor connecting two separate parts of the campus, a passageway which seemed to stretch on without end into the distance before disappearing over the horizon, apparently following rather too literally the Earth's curvature. At some point along this interminable corridor I became aware of some distance ahead the girl I'd met briefly at the disco, walking at a similar pace to me such that she never became either noticeably closer or further away no matter how I varied my speed. And so I continued involuntarily to track her (seemingly for hours) with Lisa's (for it was her) golden head always just about to dip below the horizon. Then, suddenly and quite abruptly, almost with a flourish, she was beside me. We spoke, made a date, and the rest, as they say, is history.

*

May 2020

1.08 PM
D *In case you haven't guessed I'm a bit of an armchair anarchist.....anti-government, anti-big brother snoopathon and I resent how the few control the many.... Now that I've had my eyes opened to what's going on I am quite angry about it. From the moment we are born we are told what to think, how to behave and what's true and what's not true....but they lied about that. They haven't told us the truth at all. So that's what I'm doing now...I'm on a search for ultimate truth. I happen to think I'm finding some.*

1.15 PM
L *I also am on a search for ultimate truth. If only there was such a thing, what a wonderful place the world would be.*

*

Mary always looked as if she'd been inflated, her turgid form invariably enveloped in tent-like dresses like wind-filled kaftans (Demis Roussos on steroids). Scant hair, prominent nose, large face looming insidiously, constantly doing something strange with her lower lip, some sort of nervous tic. I would examine this face in horrified fascination whenever opportunity presented. She would ask how I was occupying myself during lockdown. Managing to reign in potentially lethal levels of irritation (first it was the ghouls in Lexington, now this) at the gratuitously insulting subtext of the question, I said I'd been considering a number of options, including training courses. Training for what, she asked, with a sinister pull and twist of the lower lip. I'm looking at a number of options, I repeated. Business management. IT, possibly. And so on. None of which was true, of course.

Geoff was smaller in all respects than his wife - thin, bald, somewhat wizened, always smiling in friendly fashion while he conversed (when permitted), rarely looking directly at whoever he was speaking to, but rather thirty or so degrees to one side, with just the occasional dart of bright blue eyes from under surprisingly bushy eyebrows. In addition to being almost hairless (apart from the eyebrows) his skin was very dark-hued. Of course there may have been some interesting ethnic mix going on somewhere in his lineage, but it looked unnatural, as if he'd been varnished a number of times, getting darker with each coat to an almost mahogany shade, such that together with his large, innocent eyes, small size and strange, quick movements he always suggested to me some previously undiscovered order of lower primate - a hairless lemur variant, possibly. Scampering excitedly around the room, shrill calls of fear and warning, climbing, leaping with incredible speed up atop the furniture, or up the steep slopes of Mary's shapeless yet voluminous pitched tent of a dress to perch on her head, calling raucously, head thrust back, yet still turned thirty degrees from true, while the lower lip of his mate twisted and turned, contorting first one way and then the other as she tried furiously to remove the interloper.

*

12:43 PM
D *Well the cold virus has always killed some old people....nothing new there.....so if people think they can shut down the world for a cold virus ...well I think they need to think again! Anyway....they want the population down to 1/16th of what it is now....according to the Georgia Guidestones.....have you heard of them?*

12:49 PM
L *Sure.*

12:51 PM
D *So yeah.....they want the population down to just 500 million.....so obviously they ain't bothered if anybody*

dies, especially not the elderly....so therefore there must be another reason for the lockdown.

*

The sheer size of the game is incredible. You really could just live in it forever. Imagine a world where the only thing you hear is gunfire, explosions, and the noises of various creatures in their agonizing death throes. The devastation gives me a warm feeling of futility. Everything pretty much is dead or dying bar the endless parade of mutants, though it does make you wonder what they live on. Maybe each other.

Of course, chronologically none of it makes sense. After 210 years there would hardly be a thing left standing - the broken houses, shops, shacks, even bridges would long since have fully collapsed, turned to dust and more or less disappeared. But still I love this game in all its panoramic beauty, and that wonderful paradoxical balance common to all the best RPGs between mindless killing and problem solving. More like 'real life' than itself. Better. You never have to leave the sofa except to pee and put something in the microwave.

In fact there are times when I wish lockdown would last forever, and in perpetuity some Softshell Mirelurk is coyly hiding under rotten planking in a stinking radioactive mire before duly presenting itself to be extinguished. What could be more satisfying. Except maybe the sound of a Raider expiring. I so much enjoy killing Raiders. I particularly like it when they come apart at the seams after a burst of minigun fire. The spurting blood. So awesome. I never tire of the random noises a Raider makes going down. My cockles warmed by a merrily burning sentry bot.

*

1.20 PM
D   *Who is they, you ask? Are you telling me you aren't aware who is running the world now? Who is in the driving seat?*

1:24 PM
L   *Go on then, tell me. Who is in the driving seat? Though I will just say if the concept of a great conspiracy has meaning for you, fair enough, but it doesn't for me. It's not that there haven't been conspiracies of one kind or another throughout history, or that things don't go on that we don't know about. But a gigantic, concerted, coherent international conspiracy to control our thoughts and actions - I see no evidence for that. The constraints on human freedom throughout the world, of expression and action and opportunity, are all too obvious and explicit, and really don't need any conspiracy to explain them.*

1:32 PM
D   *I sent you that quote some time ago that speaks of the power machine....the octopus......and you dismissed it. So*

I don't see any point in telling you more when you dismissed something as important as that which was said by a President of America! Some people are so used to their prison that they no longer see the bars...

And if you missed this then I've no idea how you did.....the clues are EVERYWHERE

1:36 PM
D *If you won't believe a President who spoke about this then you sure as hell aren't going to believe me. I know when I'm beaten : -)*

1:44 PM
L *You seem incapable of giving a straight answer, and instead insist on speaking in riddles. Instead of answering my question you sidestep it by inferring that I'm some kind of an idiot for missing all the blatantly obvious clues you've strewn in my path. I think you actually enjoy the illusion of being enveloped in a cloak of mystery, some arcane puzzle to which only you have the key. I don't understand why you have to be so evasive. That is if there's any rational basis for your grand conspiracy theory.*

1:48 PM
D *I gave you that massively important quote by a President of a America that gave you the whole TRUTH*

in a nutshell.....that told you in no uncertain terms how the world is. You dismissed his words very quickly.....so why would I even bother to explain my own thoughts on it. I know when I'm flogging a dead horse and you will dismiss my words just as easily. I'm not wasting my time explaining anything to you.

1:54 PM
L Fair enough. Though that quote (I discovered) is an excerpt from The New Freedom, a 1913 book compiled from Wilson's presidential campaign speeches. And from what I've subsequently read, it's something that is often taken out of context by conspiracy theorists to 'prove' that Wilson believed in some giant sinister conspiracy. When in fact the quote talks only in vague terms of a power somewhere - nothing specific. Of course anyone can read anything they like into it, and no doubt do. But without further context and elucidation, the quote is meaningless.

2:05 PM
D I haven't read the full quote....but it changes nothing of the basic information imparted.... and only emphasises that there is no such thing as free enterprise and that you will only succeed and be allowed to prosper if THEY PERMIT IT! The rest of the quote only reinforces the fact that the powers that be have the final say and they will cut you down if your business enterprise is not one they

wish to allow.

2.24 PM
L He could be referring to the growth of Marxism and anarchism. Or maybe the increasingly unstable international situation across Europe. Or the threat to world trade from colonial revolts, separatist uprisings and nationalist movements. Or the worldwide women's suffrage movement. Or the rise of trade unionism and demands for workers' rights etc. etc. etc. etc. But the most persuasive argument is that Wilson was talking about monopolies in business, or trusts as they were called in the US. Anyway, the bottom line is that it's completely pointless to use a hundred year-old quote to substantiate a modern conspiracy theory.

2.36 PM
D The quote was not ...as you imply....referring only to the monopoly of business...... In Woodrow's quote these words were the Key Words.... 'There is a power so complete.....'

What does it mean to have COMPLETE POWER? .....ask yourself that? There's no muddiness there...Complete Power means total power....not just power in one area...a power so all-encompassing that those who speak out against it must do so under their breath!!

2.42 PM
L *I really don't think there's much point in speculating about what someone said or meant a hundred years ago. Quite a lot has happened since then.*

2.48 PM
D *To know the future it helps to know the past....and what was true then as regards the 'octopus' is only more true now....*

*

'Congratulations, Liam! Wonderful news! Absolutely delighted!' We'd somehow managed to escape Mary's vengeful eye and were chatting on a warm summer's day down the back garden. George's animated face beamed down at me from amongst the foliage as he perched high up on the branch of a mature sycamore. His eyes glowing bright blue amongst the greenery. 'I'm quite sure you'll make Lisa very happy, Liam.' I wasn't too sure about that myself, but having been swept forward by the momentum of events and my own inertia, we'd just announced our engagement. I should have voiced something of my reservations earlier, I suppose. But sometimes events take on a life of their own.

Without warning the ground began to tremble. Mary, trundling down the garden at speed carrying a long pole and with all moving parts at maximum amplitude. She came to an abrupt halt, breathing heavily and still vibrating mightily. 'Where is he? Where is he?' I believe a minor seismic disturbance was reported in the area. I'd quickly moved position beneath a different tree, just to confuse the issue and try to protect George, who I hoped was now fully concealing himself. Or possibly he'd already left the garden entirely such was his speed and agility.

I suddenly noticed Lisa's pale features surveying the scene, first from one window, then another and another, apparently somehow circling within the house like a phantom. It gave me cold shivers to see her. 'Where did he go?' 'Who?' 'Who do you think? George!' Almost choking over his name in her rage and agitation. 'I didn't see him.' The anger seamlessly transmuted into an acidic glare. 'I saw you out here talking to him.' 'Oh right, yes, but then he said he had to go to the shops and buy some bread.' 'We don't need any bread!' 'I might have misheard. Anyway, I said, Okay, see you later, got my phone out to check if I'd got any messages - hadn't - turned around and he'd gone. So I just assumed - ' But she'd already turned away in patent disgust and was now thrusting the pole viciously into as many thick clumps of foliage as she could reach. I could only hope that George had made a successful retreat. By this time the face at the windows had disappeared.

*

12.08 PM

D *There is a plan for complete world domination.... whether you choose to believe that or not is up to you.*

They already have a stronghold on everything....but they want complete domination......A one world socialist totalitarian government and one world religion...their religion.

That's the top and bottom of it but like I say, we are all free to believe what we believe and I might not agree with what you say but I defend with my last breath your right to say it!

We'll have to just agree to disagree on this....no common ground on the major issue here.

12:16 PM
L   And this brings us once more back to 'they'. And then you'll just refer me once more to Woodrow Wilson. Ever had the feeling that history repeats itself? I already know that you think that parliamentary democracy is just a front. But say it wasn't – what's the alternative? Anarchism? The devolution of power down to the lowest level? I used to believe in anarchism but I've become disillusioned with the idea. I understood that the key was the level of education. But I've come to believe that people just aren't bright enough, or well enough informed, or sufficiently motivated for that to work, at least at present. Or probably ever.

12.22 PM

D   Apparently there are two very similar groups who have this similar aim....quote:

"The ultimate objective of the leaders of both groups is identical. They are determined to win for themselves undisputed control of the wealth, natural resources, and manpower of the entire planet. They intend to turn the world into their conception of a Luciferian Totalitarian Socialist State. In the process they will eliminate all Christians, Jews, and atheists. You have just learned one, but only one, of the great mysteries."

12.26 PM

L   I don't think a socialist state is such a bad idea. At least we'd all have jobs, even if it did consist of tightening nuts in a tractor factory. It would give structure to life. A job for life, and the state looking after us. As a form of living death it's not much worse than others I could think of.

12.35 PM

D   So you think it's also a good idea to do away with the freedom of choice to be whichever religion one chooses? In fact freedom of any real kind would no longer exist....complete control of humanity is what they are after and somehow you think this is okay?????

And tightening nuts in a tractor factory ....is a living

death, indeed....and you'd see it differently if it was you who was tightening nuts month in month out with your very soul crying out for rescue!.... Your thinking processes are astounding to me!

1:09 PM
L *Well thank you, I'm flattered! But really, for one who claims to have a great sense of humour, you seem completely immune to irony. But then there are many different forms of humour. Of course I didn't mean it about tightening nuts!*

1:15 PM
D *BORN FREE......AS FREE AS THE WIND BLOWS ....AS FREE AS THE GRASS GROWS....BORN FREE TO FOLLOW YOUR HEART!*

1:26 PM
D *I do have a great sense of humour......but as yet I don't have a handle on your own sense of humour so forgive me for not realising it was said in jest. Our whole conversation thus far today has been serious so I wasn't expecting any humorous irony to be thrown in......I'm not usually slow on the uptake...pardonez moi!*

1:34 PM
D *I like these twists on the regular quotations...*
If you can keep your head when all about you are losing

theirs.....you are obviously not fully aware of the situation!!

The lamb may lie down with the lion.....but the lamb won't get much sleep...

Man goes into a butchers....asks the butcher if he's got a sheep's head...
Butcher replies 'No, it's just the way I part my hair'

Another...

Man goes into a butchers and says 'I keep thinking I'm a moth'
Butcher says 'Well that's very interesting but I'm only a butcher.... shouldn't you be going to see a psychiatrist?'
Man replies... 'I know... and I'm on my way there....but your light drew me in..'

1:45 PM
L You haven't had your head in that Ken Dodd jokebook again, have you? How many times do I have to tell you.

*

After another short but entertaining battle involving the Swan of Swan's Pond, plus various other encounters with the likes of Legendary Deathclaw (tricky) and Mister Gutsy (not difficult), I finally left *Fallout* and had a brief but satisfying flirtation with *Bum Simulator* (the title of the game a work of art in its own right), which is all about surviving the mean streets of Bumsville as a homeless guy. Okay, so you've lost half your brain (maybe more), and your speech is pretty much limited to *Ugh!* or *Ughh?* or *UgghHh!* or *Ughh!* or *Whugh?* and so on, and your best pal is a shopping cart called Carl who's lost his human body, both courtesy of experimentation by EvilWay corporation.

So the odds are stacked. But Carl has a heart of gold, and he/it guides you playing as the brain-damaged Bum through the game. You need to scavenge for food, drink, and bits of scrap to survive, so you search through garbage cans and bags of trash to find useful items which then go into your inventory held by Carl. As members of the Creeps, one of the two bum gangs who rule Bumsville, there's fights with the rival gang (the Bugs) where you get to chuck your enemies around (in fact quite a distance if you want), or spin them above your head, or shove them headfirst into garbage cans (what more could you possibly want from life), there's a Pigeon Lady who looks like a giant pigeon, a Bug spy/traitor called Bugzy, creepy Mr. Jello, the mentally unstable ex-clown who runs a junkyard, more fights, explosions, time-limited quests, a map to guide you and so on, pretty much a basic but hectic vagrant edition of *GTA*.

And it's not a bad-looking game, with reasonable buildings and cars and people walking the streets, about *GTA San Andreas* level. But best of all, for no reason whatsoever, you can literally piss all over your enemies in a huge gushing yellow geyser of piss, which when you put someone down becomes a combined victory salute/posthumous humiliation.

Hugely enjoyable, but I didn't play it for long, as my curiosity about *Mankind Divided* finally won out. And by this time I was feeling thoroughly energized through my interactions with Desdemona, with all the associated and more or less erotic speculations as to what our online back and forth might lead to.

*

10:44 AM
D   *They say Savile may have been a male witch....a warlock....He was born on Halloween and they reckon he was not buried lying down....apparently he wanted to see the sea from his final resting place! But the influence he had in high circles was the giveaway....he was obviously a lot more than Jim'll fix it or a DJ or a charity worker....a lot more to him than met the eye and it's as dark as dark can be....I mean the whole structure that kept his nefarious deeds away from the general public.*

10:59 AM
L   *Yeah I've read about him being a warlock. In fact he said as much himself - a self-confessed éminence grise who regularly wore a wizard's cloak, with his cigar as his wand, and who used magical signs and language.*

11:02 AM

D   They were merely protecting themselves through him.....he was their finder...he came in useful for them and so if he was allowed to be investigated they'd worry that their own deeds would come out, which inevitably they would have. So again we come back to ultimate power....you still going to tell me there's no big conspiracy going on and the world is really a nice, soft and fluffy place where good conquers all and there's such a thing as justice?

11:11 AM

L   I never said that, or thought it for a minute! I'm sure there are all kinds of secret agreements going on that we never know about. And mean conspiracies in high places to protect those in power and cover various misdeeds. What I think is unlikely is that there is a concerted international conspiracy to gain complete control over the world population. It would require a degree of coordination and cooperation between the interested parties, whoever they may be, which defies belief that it is possible. Human beings tend to fudge and muddle through and make stupid mistakes. A grand plan such as you're suggesting would fall apart at the seams. Put your faith in the fallibility of humans and their infinite capacity for cocking things up.

11:30 AM

D   Well again we come to the statement by Woodrow Wilson....he talks of a power that is just the kind you say there would need to be to pull it off!

A reminder: "They know that there is a power somewhere so ORGANISED, so SUBTLE, so WATCHFUL, so INTERLOCKED, so COMPLETE, so PERVASIVE....that they better not speak above their breath when they speak in condemnation of it." Arms folded......I don't think he could have put it any plainer that the power he spoke of is all powerful.

11:40 AM

D   If this power was not All Powerful....someone somewhere would have brought Jimmy Savile to justice.....but it was simply not allowed which means an awful lot of people have to be scared of the same thing that those American businessmen were scared of. You don't mess with the big boys.....and you do as we say....would have been the message given to anyone who wanted to pursue Jimmy Savile for his crimes. Those octopus arms of theirs sure do stretch wide haha

11:44 AM

L   I'm still waiting to hear who or what this person or group or entity is.

*

On later visits to Lisa's parents Mary had taken to locking George in a large refrigerator for extended periods. At least that was my belief. Of course it wasn't switched on, and several air holes had been drilled in each side, so things weren't as bad as they might have been. Nevertheless I could only imagine the anguish the poor creature must have felt being so constrained, especially given his obvious joy in roaming free among the tree tops. To be so cramped in this tiny space, barely able to stretch his limbs, must have been intolerable. I thought I could sometimes hear his voice calling as if from a distance, quietly, mournfully.

On the first visit after his incarceration I went directly to open the fridge, following the sound of his voice, and in fact had grasped the handle when Mary spun round with uncanny agility and warned me off with a tone of unmistakable menace. 'But I'm sure I can hear George in there,' I said. 'He must have climbed in for some reason and got himself trapped. We've got to get him out.' I thought it better to pretend it was an accident and ignore the obvious evidence of the air holes. 'Nonsense. He's just gone to the shops.' 'But I heard him.' 'It must be your imagination. Or an hallucination.' A veiled threat in that last remark.

I backed off, half doubting the evidence of my senses, and went out into the garden to see if I could detect any sign of Lisa's father. I scanned the trees, but saw no telltale movement among the leaves and branches, then looked back at the house, checking each window in turn. Without warning Lisa's face appeared at the window of an upstairs bedroom. Overcoming a sudden feeling of dread, I thought of waving, but her blank expression was disconcerting, and in any case she disappeared after a few seconds.

*

June 2020

9:31 AM
D *I even believe the world is flat....and I couldn't give a monkeys if people think I'm out of my tree when I say that. It's what I think and I'm never frightened to say what I think.*

9:35 AM
L *I suppose I have to ask the obvious question. What happens at the edge? Oh and related to this would I be right in thinking that you disbelieve in the moon landings, and what appear to be photographs of the Earth (a spherical Earth) taken from space?*

9:59 AM
D *Those photographs of earth are merely CGI....many different versions of them over the years.*

Aintcha seen the big ice wall on the internet? That's the edge....If gravity is so strong it can hold vast oceans in place then how come we can jump off the earth with little problem? If it's spinning at approx 700 mph then how come I can build a house of cards that a tiny waft from a door closing would topple? It feels still to me.....it looks flat to me......and I think it's one of the biggest lies they've told us...but as you know I think they've lied to us about all the important stuff.

And no I don't believe they landed on the moon....several astronauts have been quoted as saying they couldn't get through the Van Allen Belts....aka the Dome

*

On a subsequent visit the fridge had been moved, leaving a gap among the kitchen units where it had stood. Shocked, I asked what had happened to it. 'We're getting a new, smaller fridge,' came the frosty reply. 'But what happened to the old one?' 'Gone. Recycled.' Once again George's absence was explained by his apparently insatiable obsession with shopping. I didn't believe any of it, of course, and when that afternoon Lisa and her mother suggested a walk through some nearby woods, I excused myself on the grounds of a splitting headache. This was believed so readily (though without any corresponding expression of concern or sympathy) that I half suspected a set-up, and as soon as they'd gone searched for any signs of hidden bugs or cameras. Finding none, I set about combing the house for any clues to George's whereabouts.

I'd checked in almost all the other rooms when,

somewhat despondently, I came last of all to a little-used drawing room. Firmly grasping the wooden knob, shiny, rounded and old-fashioned, I turned it and pushed. The door was locked. Though I could hear nothing, even after putting my ear to the door and listening intently for several seconds, somehow I knew that George was entombed, presumably still within the fridge, on the other side. I rattled the doorknob a number of times while exerting all my strength against the locked door.

Failing to make any impression I went to the kitchen, found a wood polish and some cloths, then spent several minutes polishing the knob until it reflected the light like a mirror and I could see my face, distorted, looking back at me. As though, in my agitation and confusion, paying this absurd tribute to the dark wooden doorknob might cast some spell which would allow the door to be opened. Naturally it had no effect, and in growing desperation I gathered my strength and gave the door a number of mighty kicks that finally and with a loud crack broke the wood around the lock sufficiently that the door sprang back, hitting something behind it with force and almost rebounding in my face.

The room was dark. The curtains, drawn, were thick, allowing little light to pass through. I felt for the light switch. Finally locating it I pressed. The room remained in darkness. I subsequently discovered that the bulb had been removed. Allowing myself a few moments for my eyes to adjust, I made my way carefully towards the window and pulled back one of the heavy curtains. The room was bare, save for in one corner a bureau desk and chair, and in the other, the refrigerator. I stood stock still, staring at it for maybe ten or fifteen seconds, barely able to believe what I was seeing, even as I had been fully expecting to find it there.

I slowly approached the fridge. I couldn't remember how the door had previously been secured, but now through the handle and through a strong bracket attached to one side was a stout chain and padlock. The fridge was standing a couple of feet from the wall, such that I was able to cautiously examine it right around, wary of any booby trap. Seeing nothing suspicious, I reached out and nerved myself to touch it. Nothing happened, but as I continued to keep my hand pressed against the fridge, I thought I could detect slight movement from within.

I crouched down, and through one of the air holes whispered, 'George. George, can you hear me?' At first nothing. I repeated, 'George, can you hear me? Are you okay?' Pressing my hand once more against the fridge, this time I felt a definite movement. Then, in a faint croak, 'Liam. Is that you? Get me out of here. Please.' It was a huge relief to hear his voice, to know that he was at least still alive. Attempting to ascertain his condition, I asked how he was doing. But after a long pause there came just a repeated whispered plea to release him from his cruel confinement. I tried to reassure him, telling him I'd have him out of there in a few minutes. And it was at this point that I suddenly became aware of the passage of time and of the possible imminent return of Mary and Lisa. I leapt up and rushed outside to the garden shed where I knew there were tools. Searching frantically around the gloomy interior of the shed, there behind the lawnmower, answering my prayers, was a sledgehammer.

Clutching it, darting back into the house, I felt instantly empowered, deciding on the spot that I would use it as a defensive weapon if necessary. Warning George to stop up his ears and brace himself, it took just a couple of direct blows to the padlock to break it, then a few moments to pull the chain out. I tentatively opened the fridge door and pushed it fully back. The stench was almost overpowering. Stumbling, crawling out from where he'd been trapped, mired in his own wastes, completely naked, came a creature less recognizably human even than before. His formerly bright blue eyes, now dimmed, glanced up at me momentarily with a look that seemed to acknowledge the shame of his filthy, raw state, together with what I interpreted as an expression of gratitude.

Then, seeming to gather strength by the second, he rose up and leapt towards the window and began scrabbling furiously in an attempt to open it. 'It's okay, it's okay,' I said, attempting to calm the poor tortured soul. Guessing his intent, I quickly unlatched the window and threw it open. He sprang through the opening, loped swiftly down the garden and leapt up into the trees, climbing rapidly to the upper branches, then away and out of sight. And that was the last I ever saw of him. I like to think that he's still out there somewhere, feral but free, up in the treetops of some remote wood or forest.

After that I never again accompanied Lisa on a visit to

her parental home. And although nothing was ever said about either her father or my role in his escape, I felt a definite hardening of attitude towards me, as kissing and hugging, together with other forms of intimacy, gradually dwindled to nothing.

*

11.35 PM
D *It's Divine Law that they have to reveal the truth/their intentions....but they do it in oblique ways...only those who have the eyes to see will notice these truths that they give us.*

It's interesting, therefore, that in lots of mainstream films in the background you will see a map of the flat earth.....Hidden in Plain Sight. That is one of their mottos...hidden in plain sight....maybe that's why the United Nations flag is also a flat earth map...

11:37 PM
D *So now you can google 'Who has the motto Hidden in Plain Sight?' and you'll get to find out who I've been talking about this whole time as regards world takeover!*

11:41 PM
L *The way the UN flag is presented (like pretty much any other map) is just the obvious diagrammatic way of presenting it. I googled it. General Patton?*

11:48 PM
D *You didn't google it properly....you know who I'm referring to! I know you know!*

11:50 PM
L *Just tell me straight who you're talking about. Satanism? The Devil? I don't know.*

11:56 PM
D *I think you know a whole lot more than you are letting on about....and I'm seldom wrong haha!*

12:01 AM
L *Are you talking about the Illuminati?*

12:07 AM
D *I'm talking about the Rosicrucians, The Druids, The Freemasons, The Knights of the Round Table, The Knights of Malta, The Skull and Bones Society, The Illuminati....it's all the same thing! Just goes under different names....*

12:09 AM
L *Well, we got there in the end.*

*

As I sensed Desdemona becoming more interested in me/Uncle Eric on a personal level rather than merely an unwilling subject for her proselytizing, she began to tell me about her past or (other) ongoing dating site correspondents. There was K, for example, a Cultural Marxist with a love for stockings and suspenders and women with their tits out. I replied that I liked the sound of K (I didn't), and that she'd have to ask him sometime how the trial was going, a minor witticism which received a dead bat response. There was Stockbroker/Windmills (Stockbroker because he purported to be a stockbroker residing in a luxury pad in central London, Windmills because he was a devotee of Windmills of Your Mind) who looked great on some of his profile pics though not so much the later ones, but still he had great legs and thought she was super smart and admired her greatly and also he always had a rum and coke in his hand, and he's a real sweet guy who makes her laugh because he's daft and a chatterbox. And what about the handsome cynic Vinny of chiselled good looks and stern expression for whom she still carried a moist and excited torch and with whom she once spent two hours on the phone doing a crossword, for which cosy collaboration he gently thanked her, touching and warming her heart. From Middlesbrough, of all places (I've lived in Middlesbrough, and frankly it's the last place I'd go to find a handsome cynic, just another layer of unreality from this woman). I thought he sounded like a dick, and said so.

Then there was Jigsaw, so-called because of a

predilection for spending his leisure hours doing jigsaws (sounded highly unlikely to me, but on the other hand perhaps too unlikely for anyone to actually make it up), and who fancied her big time and loved her intelligence and quirkiness and who would sign off with 'laters gorgeous'. I can't remember now which of these losers told her never to believe a man if he tells her she's special or beautiful as all men lie and all they want is to shag as many women as they can, and that guys get bored after three shags max and move on really quickly cos it gets 'old' real quick. Then supposedly later said he was talking about other guys and how they treat women, not himself. What a prick.

At least he would have been if he'd ever existed. I later realised she was making all this stuff up as a ploy to raise her stock (she was getting on for sixty after all) and to provoke a jealous reaction in me/Uncle Eric. Did it? Well, maybe a little at first, till I realised I was being jerked around on the end of a long pole.

*

July 2020

6.53 PM
L   *Not sure I altogether buy into the theory of microchipped humans. But if you could completely disable aggressive tendencies, then society would be transformed. It all depends who's writing the code.*

7:00 PM

D *It's not a theory.....they've already started implanting people with chips. May I send you the biblical quotes and the other bit that tells that they've already started it? Won't take long to read.*

7:04 PM

D *Revelation 13: 16-18 'He forces all people, great and small, rich and poor, free and slave, to receive a mark on their right hands or on their foreheads, so that they could not buy or sell unless they had the mark, which is the name of the beast or the number of its name.*

This calls for wisdom. Let the person who has insight calculate the number of the beast, for it is the number of a man. That number is 666.'

7:06 PM

D *This is from an article I found: 'Today we see these chips already being inserted in people. As an example Sweden is known for its tech and citizens having microchips in their hands, which they use for buying selling and business.*

This ties in to what the Bible says about the microchip being used for buying and selling also, and we are told eventually everyone will be forced to take a microchip or be killed (Revelation 13:15).

Revelation 13:15 The second beast was given power to give breath to the image of the first beast, so that the image could speak and cause all who refused to worship the image to be killed.

7:08 PM
L *I've made a point of not studying the Bible. What's the context of this quote?*

7:10 PM
D Well it's prophesied that at some time in the future i.e. Now (imminent) the dark forces i.e. the Illuminati will force humanity to receive a microchip in their hand or forehead....if anyone refuses to have the microchip they will be killed, simple as that. It's the mark of the beast....Satan...so obviously anyone refusing to have it will be believers in God...and they want anyone who believes in God to be wiped off the face of the earth.

This New World Order they are ushering in....It's a One World Totalitarian Socialist Government. They are determined to bring in, one world, one currency, one religion....THEIR religion ...which is Luciferian.

7:17 PM
L *Bit of a leap equating a mark, whether on the face or the hand, with a microchip? I'm guessing the Bible doesn't use that word.*

7:20 PM
D   *Revelations is all about how we will know we are in the end times. What signs there will be that the end times are upon us.*

7:25 PM
D   *Well the microchip is used for buying and selling....and without that chip no one will be able to buy or sell anything! Of course it's the microchip....*

7:27 PM
L   *It's true the state will have absolute power when access to everything is controlled by cards and microchips. I watched a documentary about a city in China where there's a trial scheme of near total surveillance. And of course there's the social credit system of punishment/reward depending on how well you toe the line. Absolute control by card or microchip is just the next logical stage. But what's worse - a world in violent chaos, or a world that's so tightly controlled you can hardly breathe without permission, but at least you can walk the streets without fear and there's hardly any crime? The problem lies with the species itself.*

7:34 PM
D   *A young mother in America, who is poor and on government welfare tried to refuse the chip....they told her that if she did not agree to being chipped she would*

forfeit any payments......so she had no choice but to accept the chip... with young children to feed and no other income what choice did she have?

7:35 PM
D   And absolute power is their goal......they are going all out now for just that.

7:38 PM
L   But - for example - if all the individual governments of the EU were party to this conspiracy, then there wouldn't be so much or any hostility to the idea of the EU itself or loss of national sovereignty. Nor states seceding from it. Which again confounds the idea of a coherent conspiracy.

7:40 PM
D   It's like a giant game of chess....but underneath all the apparent separatism there is a coherent plan to bring in this New World Order.

*

All that stuff about people being chipped reminded me of *Human Revolution* wherein the Illuminati had plans (later subverted) to place limitations on augmented people with a biochip. And so my suspicions increased that this strange woman was merely toying with me, even as I grew ever more infatuated if more wary and even somewhat repelled by her. Thinking, maybe in reality she's an agent of some elusive anti-establishment organization. Perhaps this dating site serves as her recruiting method. But if so, why waste so much time on a sceptic like me? Because she knows that converts often become the most extreme and fanatical followers of a creed? But I have no hacking skills, so what's the point.

Of course eventually I learnt or worked out the truth - one possible/probable truth - that she was merely a deeply boring self-obsessed woman living alone in her self-created fantasy world. But still I couldn't stop looking at her photos. She was just so lush, so luscious, with more than a hint of the dissolution I've always hungered for. The eyes cold, mesmerizing, knowing. The mouth, or rather lips, wide, full, cruel, fully in control of their destiny, almost certainly versed in the finer arts of lovemaking. Was she really the age she claimed? Was it she who was writing a novel? One result of her growing interest in me was that she began to send self-written erotic stories of surpassing vulgarity and obscenity, which I took to be on the same level of reality as her stories about Stockbroker/Windmills, Jigsaw, K, Vinny et al, and whose grotesquely submissive nature both nauseated and thrilled me.

In addition to refusing to tell me her name, she also refused to tell me where she lived, except that according to her profile it was somewhere in the North East. I finally worked out via subtle clues and hints that it must be Newcastle, possibly Gateshead (what were the odds). And then a credible reason for all the cloak and dagger stuff occurred to me (other than that she was a member of some secret anti-government, anti-New World Order, anti-Illuminati organization) which was that she was in fact a member of the oldest club in the world - a call girl/escort/prostitute. Hence the veil of secrecy and concealed identity. Hence the porn-style stories. Where chatting to saps like me online was a way of killing time between clients. I once said to her, I think you just invent meaningless rules for yourself, for no known reason. Maybe there was a reason. But if so surely she wouldn't have posted images of herself. If they were of her.

*

10:40 AM
D *Haven't you heard of the 20 million club? These days anyone who is anyone is paying allegiance to the dark side. If they don't agree then they simply don't get the airplay, they don't get invited onto chat shows etc....they are not allowed to prosper big time unless they agree to the rules.....Katy Perry admitted to selling her soul to the devil....*

10.43 AM
D *The statue I was telling you about is of Baphomet....the devil...no question. I did not need to research it....it's got the goat horns! As for it being a joke....that's even laughable in itself.....I wasn't laughing when I saw it.....I was disgusted. You are not a believer...I am and it's*

disturbing to see that this dark thing is everywhere in our world.

*

It was at about this point that I decided that it might be advantageous to at least appear to agree with her outlandish theories, and pretend that she'd finally managed to convert me to her world view. At the time I was ambivalent as to whether I really was starting to be convinced by the ceaseless promotion of her 'beliefs' - such is the power of propaganda - or whether it was just a cynical attempt at manipulation on my part. Presumably a bit of both as I was unable to decide. Strangely, though, as soon as I stopped the scepticism and occasional mild mocking and began to agree with her, she abruptly dropped the evangelizing and concentrated almost entirely in our exchanges on the personal. As though she considered that her work was done - or that it was no longer entertaining without decent and disbelieving opposition.

*

I sometimes felt as if I was losing personal agency caught up in the web of her make-believe. At the same time increasingly suspecting that she was merely a fantasist, inventing these stories of sexual exploits, interweaving them with well-researched if insane conspiracy theories. And that all the reported dialogues with online pen pals were likely just as fictional as the pornographic tales she sent me. Who really was this Desdemona, about whom I knew next to nothing, not even her real name? What did she really look like? For all I knew she could have been anybody, of any age, any appearance, even any gender. Was she just playing a slightly malicious game for her own amusement, manipulating me, toying with me, treating me like some character in an RPG, taking me through the game in the direction of her own choosing.

*

Lisa asks me what I've been doing today. I reply noncommittally, not much, or something of the kind. She half smiles, equally noncommittally, then turns away to do something else. Of course I don't tell her I've spent all afternoon chatting to Desdemona. Conversations between myself and Lisa always had a curiously strained, unnatural quality - somewhat reminiscent of *Oblivion*, now I come to think of it. The lack of emotional engagement, the talking at cross purposes, the wilfully meaningless absurdity (that was mainly me). Whose fault? Nobody's. A natural outcome of discordant personalities. Resultant. Her voice we can do nothing about, unfortunately. Thin, sometimes grating, a not altogether pleasant quality.

*

We meet, exchange one chaste kiss, then never speak or see each other ever again. Think how romantic that would be. I've really come to like you a lot. Really? Well, I like you too. More than like, as you know. A caring, even. I care about you. Despite the fact we have little in common. And that we share very little in terms of beliefs. Still I care about you. Part of the reason being that you make yourself vulnerable through your honesty. I know you say you're armour-plated - maybe that's how you like to think of yourself, or want others to think of you. But underneath the armour plating there's a warm, kind woman.

It's not necessary always to believe what you say, it's only necessary to say it. And what if not only is she not what she says she is, but she's not even a woman? What if she's some young guy, a teenager even, pretending to be a woman in her late fifties. We could be two guys chatting to each other, each pretending to be something we're not, me affecting that I'm sixty and divorced, him that he's a middle-aged woman. I could even message him/her. Say something like, I have a new theory about you. Oh yes? Which is that far from being a fifty seven year old woman, you're a young guy in your twenties. And whereas I've been speculating that your name might be Laura, or Susan, or Catherine, or Loraine, I'm now thinking it's probably Luke. Or Kevin. Or Sebastian. Or James.

*

It was probably around the time I started playing *Mankind Divided* that a perverse corner of my mind began to entertain the idea that there might after all be something in D's theories of shadowy forces behind so much in the world that was evil. As there, just as Desdemona had always said, was the Illuminati - the hidden hand behind most of the dark goings-on in the game. That's the thing, if something keeps appearing with sufficient regularity, in print or any other medium, it creates its own reality. And as I say, it turns out that quite predictably they're behind most of the shit that goes down. But still, aside from that, *Mankind Divided* is a beautifully crafted, immersive work of art. Adam Jensen makes a great first person protagonist, wandering around Prague with just sufficient understated swagger, and a soft, slightly rough-edged voice that can turn menacing when necessary, the lone gunslinger who puts a stop to all some hick town's woes without raising his voice.

As to gameplay there's sufficient to the main mission to make it worthwhile, and plenty of side missions to explore. And if it doesn't quite match *Human Revolution* in that respect, it's still really good. I wasn't too keen on a couple of the voice actors - Miller and Macready in particular - but Jensen and Vega and most of the others are nicely voiced. Prague is beautiful, highly detailed, though no real advance in that respect over *L.A. Noire*. NPCs are an element of games I enjoy disproportionately, and in *Mankind Divided* they're wandering around doing all kinds of fun random stuff (sneezing, sweeping leaves, smoking cigarettes, looking at their phones, drinking from cans, taking selfies).

But the strangest thing was coming across an NPC that

looked exactly like Desdemona. I had to pause the game and save the image of it/her. Standing looking into space wearing a dark mid-length coat and knee-length boots. Comparing this image with photos of her I'd copied and saved from the dating website, they were beyond reasonable doubt the same person. What she, or at least her image, was doing in the game I can't explain.

*

I think I'm in love with you. Are you serious? Yes, of course. Are you surprised? Or maybe, Let me ask you something. Do you think it's possible to fall in love with someone you've only ever corresponded with, have never so much as spoken to, still less met, and possibly/probably never will? Are you saying you're in love with me? Umm. Not necessarily. I was proposing a hypothetical situation, and wondered what your thoughts were. Because there wouldn't be any point doing that. I know. Nothing personal, that's just the way it is. I know, you make that quite clear in your profile.

She never asked me about being a writer or what I wrote. Rather like Lisa in that respect (if no other) - a complete lack of intellectual curiosity. Apart, that is, from her non-intellectual non-rational obsessions. Or perhaps, Am I in love with you? No. No. No, of course not. No, that's a preposterous suggestion. Absolutely not. No, a thousand times no. Yes. Look, I won't embarrass you by declaring my undying love for you. If by any chance I feel an undying love for you, I'll keep it to myself. Is that okay? That's fine. Probably for the best.

*

August 2020

10:06 AM
L *So, after all this time - what's it been, four months? - and now that we're out of lockdown and all that nonsense - how's about we get down to the nitty-gritty! I reckon it's time to meet up and see what happens. What do you say?*

10:23 AM
D *Well now, I don't know about that :-)*

10:26 AM
L *Come on, you know you want to!*

10:31 AM
D *You're pretty sure of yourself, aren't you! But like I've said many times before - and once more I refer you to my profile - I'm only here for the chat. I just don't really meet people as a rule.*

10:34 AM
L *You told me once you were going to meet Vinny for a night of unbridled passion.*

10:45 AM

D   *Yes, that's true, but I didn't in the end. My self-respect kicked in at the last minute!*

10:47 AM

L   *Self-respect should never get in the way of self-realization.*

10:48 AM

D   *I just decided I was better than that.*

10:52 AM

L   *His loss, no doubt. But I'm not asking for that. Just to meet and chat. I'd love to hear your voice. I haven't even spoken to you on the phone, unlike cousin Vinny. I'd really like to be able to look at your face while we chat of this and that and the other.*

10:58 AM

D   *Oh, so you fancy a bit of the other now do you haha?!*

11:04 AM

L   *If it's on the menu! But no, not necessarily - I'm interested in you for yourself, because I find you interesting.*

11:09 AM

D   *I have to say you make that sound somewhat underwhelming ha….*

11:10 AM
L *Okay, very interesting!*

11:13 AM
D *That's better! Now that didn't hurt, did it!*

11:15 AM
L *So what's the answer?*

11:22 AM
D *Let me think about it*

*

How exactly was I going to respond when she first sees me and after a long moment of confusion and disbelief asks in an icy tone where I obtained the anti-aging pills? Or would it be me asking the same question, coupled with a follow-up query relating to gender. So many unknowns, so many variables, so many lies. So many fantasies and evasions. We'd already exchanged all the usual stuff, childhood, family, and in my case, children. Both grown up and moved away now, of course.

The eldest, Lucy, about to have a child of her own. My first grandchild, Faustus (I'd already been informed of the gender). Lucy, an aggressive tearaway through her teens, now about to become a mother. I almost pitied poor Faustus, but who knows, maybe his mother would grow into her maternal role. Then there's Huxtable, two years younger than Lucy, a studious, pacific young man working towards his PhD. It would be difficult to imagine two more disparate personalities, but fortunately they get on well together, Lucy always highly protective of her little brother.

And so it went on, enriched with corroborative detail, filled with anecdotes of childhood escapades, mainly my own masquerading as the hi-jinks of Lucy in particular, occasionally Huxtable. And Desdemona responded in kind with her/his own make-believe back story. An aging mother with a penchant for dirty jokes. An older sister who thinks she's the best thing since refined petroleum. A neighbour in the flat above who refuses to turn down his hi-fi or take the hint even when she screams at the top of her voice.

*

I went against my instincts as Adam Jensen and employed a non-lethal approach most of the time, relying instead on stealth to work my way through missions. Which tends to pay off as suspects provide information which you'd never get if you just killed them straight away. And there's plenty of weapons and augmentations you can add to Jensen's inventory, though the Glass-Shield Cloaking System made achieving missions a little less challenging than they might have been. Illuminati agents everywhere (with sickly inevitability), up to no good as usual.

*

10:24 PM
D *Okay, so it's a go*

10:51 PM
L *Is that a yes??!!*

11:01 PM
D *No, it's a go haha*

11:03 PM
L *So, just to be clear, does that mean we're going to meet up?*

11:07 PM
D *You're a bit slow today aintcha, Liam! Yes. we're going to meet up*

11:10 PM
L *Awesome! Where?*

11:15 PM
D *Do you know Blakes? On Grey St in central Newcastle*

11:17 PM
L *Yeah, I know it. Sounds perfect. When?*

11:20 PM
D *When are you free?*

11:21 PM
L *Saturday? Say 2pm?*

11:29 PM
D *Yeah that's fine*

*

I didn't notice anything amiss at the time, so excited was I was at the prospect of finally meeting Desdemona, and all that might lead to. Only later, after reading over the brief exchange again and again until it became inscribed on my memory, was I slightly disturbed by the almost total absence of exclamation marks, a clear indicator of unenthusiasm. She'd dropped even a period at the end of each brief and uninvolved sentence - even the effort of putting a full stop was too much for her and/or too strong an indication of engagement and enthusiasm. Looking at her messages again (and again, and again) it now seemed clear that they were quite deliberately calculated to demonstrate minimum interest and involvement. Or perhaps minimal interest or involvement plus a healthy dose of evasion would naturally result in precisely the cool, cursory effect achieved.

Of course I was reading far too much into it. She was probably just busy with something while she messaged, probably making a meal for her elderly, housebound mother while trying to remember another suitably filthy joke from her Ken Dodd jokebook. I had a sudden vision of her, dressed exactly as she was in *Mankind Divided*, walking into Blakes, her lips still moving as she rehearses another ancient witticism. But then without warning she shapeshifts into a pasty, rat-faced teen, sneaking around the tables, trying not to be seen.

*

So this was it, at last. We'd finally reached endgame. Or was it just the beginning of some serious gameplay. Which, if I was being honest with myself, and putting literary ambition to one side for the moment, was what I really desired. Why then, as I walked down Grey Street on a warm summer's day, surrounded by shoppers and tourists enjoying the sunshine, did I feel sick to my stomach with tension. No doubt for precisely the reason stated earlier - that I wasn't sixty and didn't look anything like my late Uncle Eric. And therefore would have some heavy-duty explaining to do if Desdemona was what she purported to be. The other possibility being that she/he really was a young man, perhaps with an aching, untameable desire for a physical encounter with a mature older man like Uncle Eric, a man who would take charge and lay down the rules and prosecute them forcibly. Of course that's why he'd given himself the profile of an older woman, obtaining from some source or other images of a highly attractive middle-aged woman, just the kind of woman who might appeal to a Paul Hollywood lookalike. But what did he expect to happen when, instead of a curvy up-for-anything mature female, Uncle

Eric learned to his disbelief and mounting anger that Desdemona was a pimply teenage youth.

*

So, what if Paul Hollywood and Uncle Eric were ever to meet, would they simply cancel each other out? And what if Desdemona were to marry Windmills, then divorce him and marry David Icke, would she then be Desdemona Windmills Icke? What if the world was indeed flat and was taken over by a secret cabal of reptilian shapeshifters? Would they all fall off the edge, or would they be saved by Illuminati agents? What if Jimmy Savile came back as Prince Andrew's double and was put in charge of the NHS? What if Woodrow Wilson won the decathlon at the next Olympics? What if Ken Dodd was Vinny's first cousin removed? These and other interesting questions we could explore at length if I was I and she was really she.

*

Blakes was busy, but there were a few spaces as lunchtime drifted towards afternoon tea. I found a corner seat that gave me a full view over the whole café and the windows on both Grey Street and the adjoining lane. I'd arrived twenty minutes early to anticipate the arrival of Desdemona. I'd scanned and dismissed those already seated in the café, so now my full attention was on anyone entering or hovering indecisively outside. The minutes ticked by as various groups and individuals came and went. Two o'clock. Quarter past. By half two I was feeling sick once more, but this time with self-disgust. I waited until three, then rose and left the café, aware only of the utter emptiness and pointlessness of my existence. As I walked I tried to decide whether I cared enough to bother loathing myself as much as I deserved, while at the same time feeling a hatred of murderous proportions developing for whoever or whatever had incited this humiliation.

*

Back at the flat I didn't see the note at first. The place was strangely silent. All my attention was focused on finding out what the creature had to say for her/him/itself. I opened my laptop and logged on. There were no new messages. I clicked on existing messages, and for a moment thought I must have clicked the wrong button. Desdemona had disappeared. A few other people with whom I'd exchanged an occasional desultory message were still there, but of Desdemona and all our conversations over four months there was no sign. In frantic haste I searched for her profile. But like a glitch in a game, she'd vanished without trace. And it was at this point, as I was on my way to the kitchen to grab some alcohol, that I came across the note left by Lisa. She'd obviously used my laptop for some reason, and come across the dating website. Logging on wouldn't have been difficult, as against all IT protocols and out of sheer laziness I tended to use the same password for all occasions.

You little shit. I hope you had a wonderful time with your girlfriend. What a silly pretentious bitch. And a bit old for you, isn't she? But then I never realised you were quite that old yourself. Anyway each to their own, I've been wanting to get away from you for a long time, so thanks for giving me the perfect incentive to end this so-called relationship. Don't ever try to contact me. I'll send someone round for my things. Maybe you'll appreciate what you had when you haven't got it anymore. Knowing you, probably not.
Bye forever,
Lisa

*

If anything can be thoroughly degrading, it will be. That is the great, and only, universal truth. Dear Lisa. Dear pretty seemingly innocuous Lisa. You had to know her to dislike her. But let's be clear, I'm far from being in love with myself. I do regret some of the things I've done and choices I've made. In fact truth be told I absolutely fucking hate myself. No doubt with good reason. Though to be fair my life has been fifty shades of shit. Anyway, that was it, that was how it all went down. A year ago. Time, the great healer. And so it goes. And so on. I sometimes have my doubts the woman ever really existed. Desdemona, I mean. She was probably always just a phantom, a mirage, a trick of the light. Oh and my name is not Liam. Btw.

The Church

We've bought a brand new Austin Maxi! Dad's picking it up from the dealer today. It arrived a few days ago and it's just gone to be undersealed. He'll be home in a few minutes, then after tea we're going straight out to church for a practice and I'll be able to have my first ride in the new car. Dad said it had to be a family car with at least four doors as there's four of us and not something too slow or old-fashioned like a Morris Minor or Austin Cambridge. We looked at loads of brochures that we'd picked up at dealers, Ford Cortina, Escort estate, the Viva range. Even the Herald 13/60 estate even though it's pretty old-fashioned, and loads of others.

Anyway in the end we decided on a Maxi as it's modern and has loads of space without being too big. Originally dad said he was thinking of a neutral colour like light brown or beige that wouldn't show the dirt too much. So we looked through the colour list, you can get them in yellow, red, white, blue, beige, even black. In the end we chose red with a black interior which I think looks fantastic, almost like a sports car.

The Maxi is known as 'All the fives' because it's got five doors, five seats and five gears. Having five gears in a family car is very unusual. Another slant on the five theme is, 'Become a five car family. For the price of a single Maxi.' The five cars in one being family saloon, estate car, school bus, removal van, and overnight camper - you can fold the front seats and the back seat down to make a double bed. It's got a brand new 1485cc overhead camshaft engine that they've just developed called the E-series. It produces 74 bhp at 5500 rpm and it's got a five-bearing fully counterbalanced crankshaft fitted with external vibration damper and also a ribbed aluminium rocker cover that looks great. With the engine transversely mounted and hydrolastic suspension it's similar to other designs by Issigonis like the Mini, 1100 and Landcrab.

Since I got back from school after something to eat I've been playing on the piano ready to go to church and practice the piece on the organ I'm working on. I've been given a new piece to learn by Mr Hall who's the organist at St. Luke's. He's been the organist there since the thirties when he was just a young man. His fingers are stubby and thick and always grubby from gardening and yellowed from smoking, which he does all the time except when he's actually in church. He smokes Craven A and has a real smoker's cough which sounds very loud in church. Even when he's at the console playing the organ you can hear it and it sort of punctuates his playing. His voice is gruff and deep and bronchitic, but always friendly.

Mr Hall's been teaching me the organ for about a year. Before that I learnt the piano with Miss White who was very old and frail. I used to go to her house and have my lessons in the front drawing room on a black grand piano. Her voice quavered when she spoke, and she always had a cup of tea during the lessons which was brought to her by her companion who looked as old and frail as she was. I thought at first they were sisters but later realised they weren't. When she played through my pieces she always made loads of mistakes but never seemed to notice. When I was playing she would lean in close to correct me or scribble some direction in wavering writing on the score, which I wasn't keen on as I could smell her stale breath. I far prefer being taught by Mr Hall who's humorous and also an old friend of my dad's from before the war. Dad was in the choir then and Mr Hall was the assistant organist. So they always have a joke together when dad brings me for my lessons.

The piece I'm learning is called Cantilène Pastorale by Guilmant. It's not difficult to play except at certain times you've got to hold a chord or sometimes a single note down with your right hand, then reach down to the manual below with the fingers or thumb of the same hand to play some more notes. I've got my own set of keys for the church and the organ so I can go and practice whenever I want. A couple of days ago I went down by myself in the evening to practice the Guilmant and ended up being frightened to death.

It was just turning dusk, and it was already gloomy inside the church. There was nobody else there at that time of day, so I locked the door after me. There was just sufficient light to make my way up the nave to the choir where the console is, just behind one side of the choir stalls which face each other. I switched on a single church light, then unlocked the console, lifted back the wooden cover, then folded back the glass-panelled front sections. When you first open the console it gives off a sweet not unpleasant smell. I don't know if it's partly the wood and partly because of Mr Hall's fingers stained with nicotine. Anyway the keys which are made of ivory are also slightly yellowing, at least the ones in the middle that are played most often. With a different key I unlocked the door of the box that contains the on/off buttons of the electric blower and pressed the on button. At once there was the sound of the blower starting up in the organ loft and the crackle of the bellows inflating, and then just the background humming and hissing noise of the organ brought to life.

The organ is a three-manual Harrison and Harrison, built new for the church in 1922. It's a beautiful instrument with a lovely rich sound and some gorgeous solo voices like the Claribel, Viola da Gamba, Clarinet, and on the Swell the Hautbois, a 16' stop which gives real body and depth to Full Swell, but also with Octaves Alone can be used as a solo stop without transposing. Then there's other stops like the Hohl Flute and Stopped Diapason on the Great which if you're playing a quiet piece can be used as solo stops as they're of lovely quality. The Choir and Swell are enclosed so there's two crescendo pedals which you have to remember to fully open when you finish playing so that the temperature inside the Swell and Choir boxes is equalised with the ambient temperature of the building. This helps prevent the pipes going out of tune too quickly. Even though I'm only really beginning to learn how to play the organ I love experimenting with the registration by mixing tone colours.

After playing a couple of pieces including the Guilmant it was completely dark outside, which meant it was also completely dark inside apart from the pool of light around the console area, with in addition an old-fashioned lamp on the console to illuminate the score. The great body of the church was in total darkness. Of course I could have put more lights on but I always felt I should use as little electricity as possible. I've begun to deputise for Mr Hall at some of the simpler services like the midweek Lenten services which are organ only with no choir and I've also just started to play for the occasional Evensong when Mr Hall fancies the evening off. So I feel I'm just about earning my free access to the organ, but still I think I shouldn't have all the lights in the church blazing away unnecessarily.

I was already getting quite nervous being in the darkened church by myself. After practising the tricky bits of the Guilmant a couple more times I decided to have a go at one of the Sketches for Organ by Schumann which are beautiful pieces I've been learning on the piano. I wanted to try to add the pedals to the manual parts. I was practising Sketch no.3 which is played mainly on Full Swell apart from a quieter middle section. When the organ's loud you can't hear anything else going on in the church. Somebody would have to be talking loudly in your ear even to be heard. So you don't know if there's other sounds going on or somebody coming up behind you. It's enough to make your imagination go crazy. Which it did, so that by the end of the Schumann I was terrified.

I couldn't bear to stay in the church any longer, and my only thought was to get out, which involved the long walk down the length of the nave in near total darkness. Of course I could have gone down, switched all the lights on, then gone back and turned the light by the console off. But I didn't want to have to walk up and down the church again even with the lights on. So now with the organ turned off and closed up, and all the lights switched off, and after allowing my eyes a few seconds to adjust, in a state of barely suppressed terror I began walking. And by not looking to either side but keeping my vision fixed straight ahead, and by trying to think of anything but the darkness pressing in from either side, I somehow managed to make my way to the door. Now in a frantic state I eventually fumbled the door key into the lock entirely by feel, opened the door and escaped into the fresh air, quickly and fearfully shutting and locking the church door behind me. I began walking slowly home, feeling shaky but in a state of utter relief, though with the thought of the still dark and ominous church still looming large in my imagination. Anyway, although I didn't tell dad the story, that's the reason I asked if he'd like to come down with me this time.

It's here! I'm going out to have a look at it. Dad's just parked it in the drive. It looks fantastic! A wonderful bright red colour. Everything's so perfect. And there's so much room inside. It smells amazing with that new car smell. It also smells a bit of the underseal and you can see underneath where it's been coated everywhere. Lucy's just come running out to look at it. She's my five-year-old sister. She's just jumped into the driver's seat and she's pretending to drive it.

I was eight when Lucy was born. It was strange suddenly having a little sister after being the only child. When she was little she used to cry and scream all the time. Then when she got a bit older she used to get hold of some of my favourite books and scribble on the pages with pens and crayons which was really annoying. I used to complain to mum for letting her do it when I was at school, but mum said it had only happened a couple of times and anyway I shouldn't leave my books lying around everywhere. Which I don't, they're all mainly in my bedroom. Anyway she seems to have stopped doing that now she's started school. Sometimes I play with her out in the back garden with the bikes or some of my toy cars, not the best ones, and sometimes we watch Blue Peter and the Magic Roundabout together.

Mum's just called us in for tea. We're having fish fingers, mashed potatoes and peas. Mum's recently started an Open University degree in Humanities. She's planning on becoming a teacher when she's completed it. Dad really supports the idea and is always interested in what mum's studying and always reads her essays. He always says that mum is much brighter than he is. Mum and dad discuss the day's events while we have tea. Dad talks about what happened at the office and about his friend Smithy and his funny self-drawn cartoons which are usually caricatures of people in the office. Dad says they're so good he shouldn't be wasting his time working in an office, he should be doing topical cartoons for one of the big newspapers. We're having tapioca for pudding which I absolutely hate. But at least when we're finished I'll have my first ride in the new car!

Just arrived at church. The Maxi is really smooth and quiet, though dad says the gearchange is occasionally a bit stiff and difficult to engage, maybe because it's a brand new car. I almost don't want to get out. I just love that new car smell. The car looks amazing - it's taken on a strange colour in this light, kind of a purple. Dad's just locking it. The church is almost completely in darkness. It always looks old and huge and a bit forbidding in the dark, though in fact it was only built just after the First World War, but the stone they used wasn't very good as it was too soft, so the building hasn't weathered well and is generally in poor repair. It's got side aisles and transepts, and a large central tower with a clock, but no spire. Because of its architectural style and poor condition dad always says it looks like a medieval French church.

Just in the porch unlocking the door. I always feel a strange kind of otherworldly feeling coming into church. There's still just a little light coming through the windows so I'm not turning the nave lights on, I'll just turn the one on by the console as usual. I'm not scared of being here at all now dad's with me. The church looks beautiful with the stone arches to the side aisles and the vaulted ceiling and ahead of us the east window. The organ lives up in a loft in the north transept. I've been up there once and seen all the pipes and the blower and bellows. When the blower's switched on the organ becomes a living, breathing thing.

I'm starting off with the Guilmant. I've got the tricky sections fairly fluent now. It's sounding really good.

Now I'm going to practice a couple of pieces by Jehan Alain. I'm not doing these with Mr Hall, I'm just working on these by myself. The first piece I'm doing is Postlude pour l'Office de Complies which is very quiet and mysterious. In fact it's so atmospheric that although it's fanciful I always think when I play it you can smell the incense and see wafts of smoke rising to the ceiling.

Just finished playing Litanies, the best-known of Alain's organ works. It's loud at the end, almost full organ, and it always takes a good two or three seconds for the final chord to die away. Now there's a silence that also sounds really loud, which is a strange effect.

If dad wasn't here I'd be really scared right now. Turning to my right I can see where he often sits to listen, somewhere on the front row of the pews. There's just enough light, but very quickly complete darkness beyond. He's not there for some reason. It's strange as he usually comes up to the console when I've finished playing a piece and we have a chat about it.

Dad still hasn't appeared.

The church makes strange noises from time to time. You don't really hear them during the day as there's often some activity in the church, the verger or cleaners or flower arrangers, and also traffic noise from outside. But in the evening you notice everything, the whirring and chiming of the clock, or an occasional creaking or sudden quiet click or crack of the wood of the roof or the choir stalls expanding or contracting. Or somebody walking along the choir stalls. I have to look behind me quickly and check. A cold stab of fear.

Dad won't have gone outside to have a cigarette, which is what he often does if we manage to get to play on a different organ somewhere. But here I always lock the church door behind me in the evening so that nobody can just wander in off the street, even though the church is left unlocked during the day.

Calling hello into the darkness. No reply.

Maybe he's down at the far end of the church for some reason and he'll appear in a few moments. There's a bookstall down there with various religious booklets and postcards and so on.

Getting down from the organ bench and going round between the choir stalls so that I can look down the church. Though you can't see anything much.

Calling again

Silence

Now I'm beginning to feel really scared because I don't understand what's going on or where dad's gone. The church is completely quiet and dark. Looking back at the console to see if dad's appeared there. As usual it looks like it's in a spotlight with darkness all around. Nobody's there.

Seems to be nobody here at all except me. But that's impossible.

Decided to start walking down the middle of the central aisle. Keeping as far away from everything as I can. The church now almost completely black.

There's somebody or something there. So scared now.

It must be dad. It can't be anybody else but why doesn't he reply.

All the light switches for the nave are at the far end of the church.

I don't understand where he can have gone.

Walking down the nave. The church is cold but I'm sweating with fear. Feeling almost paralyzed somehow making myself walk. The darkness is everywhere all around me.

Completely dark now. I can't see anything at all further down the church. Making myself keep walking.

I just know there's something there

Almost at the end of the lines of pews

If I can just reach the light switches

What was that   can't see anything   something moved

There's a

Please God   no

Screaming

The Decision

Laura leaned back in her chair, away from the oppressive screen, rubbed her eyes for several seconds, then groaned softly. Then gave a big sigh.

'Oh…Oh dear…Oh God…Oh dear God…'

Arthur (so named by semi-literate parents after Arthur Dent, to his ongoing dismay) looked across at Laura, and as was his wont whenever discretion allowed, took in her tall, athletic frame and mass of chestnut hair.

'Anything wrong?'

She glanced across at him and smiled.

'Oh sorry, was that out loud?'

'I'm afraid so.'

'Oh, well…just the usual.'

'Boredom?'

'Oh yes.'

'Extreme boredom?'

'Yep.'

'Lassitude?'

'Yay', in a tired, dispirited tone.

'Feelings of combined frustration, hopelessness and anger?'

'Yes…yes, certainly all of those.'

'You know, you should just walk away.'

'I have to escape. I have to break out. I just can't go on with this…this nonsense,' waving her hand languidly, encompassing indiscriminately her desk, computer screen and the office as a whole, maybe even the world, possibly even the universe. 'Why does life have to be like this?'

'Your work is good. At least so I've heard.'

'I wish that mattered to me. Let's face it, a trained chimp could do this job, probably better than at least half the people here.'

'You could just walk away.'

'It's the boredom. That's the worst thing. The almost infinite boredom.'

'You could always walk away.'

'It's the lassitude.'

'Extreme lassitude.'

'Yes, and the feelings of combined frustration and helplessness.'

'And anger.'

'And anger.'

'You could just walk away.'

'Did I mention the boredom?'

'You know, you could always walk away.'

'It's not that simple.'

'Yes it is. You just get up, gather your stuff together, and walk out.'

'I can't. I couldn't.'

'You can and you could. You're young. If the job really oppresses you that much you should just do it. Don't waste your life. Just walk out of the building and never look back.'

'You're hardly old yourself. Aren't you therefore by the same token wasting yours?'

'Forties. Divorced. That's old, relatively.'

'Nonsense.'

'Well, commitments, at least, that you presumably don't have. A son. A daughter. A mother.'

'I have a mother.'

'But of course, the question then is, what would you do instead?'

Laura's phone rang.

'Sorry, just a minute. Yes, hello? No, I'm sorry, that's quite impossible. No, that's simply out of the question. No. No. Look, we've been through all this before. I'm sorry, I'm afraid we're going to have to leave it there.'

She ended the call and threw the phone back down on her desk.

'Your mother?'

'Yes. I do wish she wouldn't phone me at work.'

'Okay, so, given a clean slate, the opportunity to do anything you wanted…'

'I…well, that's the problem, isn't it.'

'Come on. Clear blue sky. No preconceptions. Where, at this very moment, would you most like to be? And doing what?'

'Apart from sitting here talking to you while quietly emoting?'

'Precisely.'

'I think…'

'How old are you, by the way, if you don't mind me asking?'

'Twenty three.'

'To be so young.'

'I feel at least three times that. As you said, it's all relative.'

'I interrupted you. Go on.'

'I think...I'm thinking - a little cottage in the middle of nowhere, surrounded by oak woods, with nearby a clear, tinkling stream. There would be - '

'The storm went by, the sun rose bright. The lonely cot was there.'

'Yes, a lonely cot' (in a slightly irritated tone). 'And in the garden would be hollyhocks, and primroses, and pansies, and Sweet William. And fragrant herbs, and - '

'So what would you actually do in this lonely cot?'

They were interrupted by Jenny, Laura's flatmate and work colleague, appearing as if by magic from behind them.

'Hi! What are you two doing for lunch?'

'Dinner.'

'Whatever.'

'I don't know. I hadn't thought about it.'

'Fancy the pub?'

'Well, I - '

'Okay, see you there in, what, ten?'

'Fine', in a resigned tone.

Jenny smiled, waved, and disappeared back to wherever it was from whence she came.

'She's your flatmate, isn't she?'

'Jenny. Yeah.'

'How do you two get on?'

'Oh, she's not a bad old stick.'

'Must be about your age.'

'Yeah. But the thing is it's always a mistake to share a flat with someone you also work with. With whom you also work. You can never get away from them.'

'Oppressive?'

'To a degree. And she has some strange habits.'

'Oh really? Do tell.'

'Well, for instance, I decide to go to bed, and she's sitting there in the living room nursing the remnants of a large glass of wine, claiming to be exhausted and that she'll also be going to bed in five minutes, max. And yet, no sooner have I laid my head upon the pillow and started to think vague consoling thoughts, than the knocking begins. What is she knocking? And with what? What is there to knock at or with at midnight that can't be deferred till morning? And then the knocking becomes a banging, and occasionally a crashing, with the odd moan or cry thrown in. And I'm thinking, what in God's name is the woman doing?'

'You don't think she's - '

'I do hope not.'

'So how long does this combined knocking, banging and crashing not to mention moaning and crying go on for?'

'For how long do I have to endure this cacophony?'

'Yes.'

'It seems like hours. It's probably only ten, fifteen minutes. But in the dead of night - '

'Yes, I can imagine that must be quite - '

'Then there's her rugby playing boyfriend. Ray, or Reg, or Ron, or something similar. In any case a substantially proportioned individual. Not that I'm jealous, far from it.'

'What's he like?'

'Well, let's just say she can't mention his name, whatever it may be, without also mentioning the width of his chest, the width of his thighs, the width of his brow, and so on and so forth.'

'Oh dear oh dear.'

'Exactly. It's possible to have too much of that kind of thing.'

'Have you ever met him?'

'He calls for her at the flat from time to time. I try to keep a safe distance. Which is as close as I care to get.'

'Well, shall we adjourn from all this frenetic non-activity and go and join your friend…'

'Jenny.'

'Yes, Jenny.'

'Yes, I suppose so. After all, what does any of it matter.'

'That's the spirit.'

'What do you think?'

Laura was sitting quietly contemplating in the living room of the flat she shared with Jenny, a novel opened but unread on her lap. She looked up briefly as Jenny stood expectantly before her, hair newly coloured.

'Very nice.'

'Not too dark?'
'No, it really suits you.'
'What do you think of my lashes?'
'I don't know.'
'You haven't looked at them.'
Laura reluctantly glanced up once more.
'Prominent.'
Jenny laughed.
'You do say some funny things sometimes. No, really, what do you think?'
Laura exhaled audibly.
'I think they look very…pretty. That's it, very, very pretty.'
'You think they suit me?'
'Yes. Yes, I do.'
'So do I. I really think they make my eyes look big.'
Pause.
'Oh, by the way, did you remember the toilet rolls?'
'They're in the cupboard…next to the…umm…'
'Toilet?'
'Yes.'
'Do you know what I really fancy?'
Pause.
'No.'
'I really fancy spending an at-home day of pampering sometime very soon. A whole day just indulging myself to the absolute max. What do you think?'
Laura, wishing desperately to be deep in thought, and trying at least to give that impression, made no reply.
'What do you think, Laura?'

Laura sighed irritably.

'I think you should do it, if that's what you want to do.'

'We could do it together. Have a real girly day just - '

'I don't think that's such a good idea.'

'Why not?' said Jenny, her expression and voice suddenly crestfallen.

Laura decided to temporarily give up her attempt at contemplation and devote herself instead to this meaningless conversation.

'Well, I just think it's something that you should do. But alone. Or with Ron. Now there's an idea.'

'My boyfriend's called Ray, as you well know. Why do you always call him by the wrong name?'

'Oh, I'm sorry. My mind is on other things at the moment. Other than Ray, I mean.'

'What sort of things?'

'Well, I'm in something of a state of flux.'

Jenny, confused, made no response.

'I mean I need to make a decision. About my future.'

'Why, what are you thinking of doing?'

'Well that's the question. I need to make some life decisions concerning what I really want to do with my life. That or rather those kind of decisions.'

'Aren't you happy with your life?'

'I'm really very happy with my life in certain isolated aspects. But, you know, one sometimes reaches a point of feeling an irresistible urge for change.'

'I'm completely happy with my life.'

'Well, that's good.'

'I can't really imagine not being happy.'

'That's wonderful.'

'I think the only thing that could possibly make it any better would be if Ray proposed. That would just be the icing on the cake.'

'How is Ray, by the way?'

'Oh, he's great. He's never ill, you know.'

'Isn't he?'

'No, never. I think it's because he's so strong he just throws it off.'

'That must be wonderful for him.'

'Yes, I sometimes ask him, Do you never get ill, Ray? And he replies, No, never. And so I say, Have you never had even a day's illness? And he says, No, not even so much as an hour. And I say, That's quite incredible. And he replies, Yes, it is, isn't it. Not that he displays any great pride about it. I think for Ray it's just a matter of fact and an indication of his extraordinary - '

'He's really something.'

'He is, isn't he. Did I tell you he's playing this Saturday?'

'I think you did mention it.'

'They say the team's not the same without him.'

'No?'

'No.'

Arthur, delayed by apathy and a failure to correctly set his alarm, arrived around half an hour late to the office.

'Hello.'

She paused in her activity and looked across at him.

'Oh hi.'
'What are you doing?'
'I'm clearing my desk.'
'What? Why?'
'I've decided to take your advice, quit my job and start my life afresh.'
'But...'
'In fact I've decided to go home to mother, so to speak. To regroup, recharge my batteries, and then rise like the proverbial phoenix from the ashes of my former self, and create for this new self a completely new persona. I thought I might aim to be the female equivalent of Ray.'
'Who?'
'Jenny's boyfriend.'
'I thought you didn't like him.'
'I don't. It was just an idea. It doesn't have to be Ray.'
'But this is madness. Or to put it another way, are you out of your freaking mind?'
'But you're the one who told me to just walk away.'
'Don't listen to anything I say. What do I know. I know nothing.'
'You said I should just get up, gather my stuff together, walk out and never look back.'
'That's complete and utter rubbish, and in fact doesn't sound at all like the sort of thing I'd ever come out with. Did I really say that? Yes? Well if I did, it was a remarkably stupid thing to say. I honestly think you should reconsider. Stay and work things through. It's never a good idea to run away from your problems. Besides...'

Laura took in his serious expression.

'Besides what?'

And so he found himself facing one of those rare moments in life where one's destiny lies wholly in one's own hands (not strictly true, of course, with another party involved, but close enough). Sadly, put to the test, his nerve failed him. In any case he felt it would be mere self-indulgence to say anything.

'Oh, nothing…So are you really going?'

'Why? Do you think I should stay?'

'No. No, you should of course do what is best for you.'

'Well, then…' She sighed. 'I suppose I won't miss much about this place…I'll miss our little chats though.'

'Yes. Me also.'

She sighed again.

'Well, I think that's just about everything.'

'What about your notice? Have you told them? Haven't you got to work a couple of weeks' notice at least?'

'I probably should. And I probably should have told them. But following your advice I've decided just to go, to walk out without telling anyone, except you. And Jenny, of course.'

'I don't know what to say.'

'I'll be in touch.'

'Yes. Yes, let me know how you're getting on.'

'I will. Well, I guess this is it. This is where I just up and leave. Just walk out of the building and never look back.'

He doesn't reply, and she doesn't move. He feels as if the ground is opening up beneath him at exactly the same moment as his heart is being ripped from his body without anaesthetic.

The pause continued until at last, both of them standing silently facing each other, Laura spoke, haltingly.

'Well, goodbye doesn't seem to cover it. But anyway, bye for now. I'll be in touch.'

'Yes, goodbye Laura. Take care…'

A few minutes later his fathomless despair was invaded by Jenny. He looked up reluctantly.

'Where's Laura? I thought I'd see what you two were doing for lunch.'

'She's gone.'

'Gone?'

'Cleared her desk. Walked away. Never to return.'

'I didn't think she meant it. I didn't think she'd go through with it…And she never said goodbye.'

'She said you were with some people. It would have meant a scene with everyone overhearing. So she just slipped out quietly. She said she'd be in touch.'

'It's all very strange. And I'll have to find a new flatmate now. Or move in with Ray. Or maybe see if he'll move in with me.'

'I'm sorry.'

'No, it could all work out for the best. Ray sometimes just needs a little push.'

'Well, that's good then, I suppose.'

'Still it is strange her just leaving like that…Anyway, I must get on. I'll text Ray.'

After Jenny had left he looked across at Laura's empty desk. Then, after turning off his screen, he stared down at his own desk for a moment before clutching his forehead and shielding his eyes.

'Oh…Oh dear…Oh God…Oh dear God…'

Kira

1

'The path has no meaning for you,' said my mother. 'You are not to go down it.' She would repeat the same formula (with slight variations) several times over like an incantation. 'The path has no meaning. Do not go down it.'

Of course nothing is more intriguing to a child than that which is forbidden, the eternal lure of the unknown and taboo. We knew that the path referred to by my mother led out of the village to a strange circular building occupied by Superions, and (it was rumoured) beyond that to the City. But there was another path, also forbidden, that led into the forest.

'Now shoo! Outside with you, and let me get some work done in the house before I go into the fields. I'll bring you all out a snack in a little while. But remember what I said about the path.'

And finally she picked us up one by one with her strong yellow teeth - me, my younger sister Marja, and my best friends Miza and Olean - and deposited us in the garden outside like so many naughty kittens.

Kira was a smiling, happy girl, slim and tall for her age. Now coming up to twelve. I talk of myself as if I were somebody else entirely. It's easier to describe what happened as if I'm looking at myself doing these things.

'You're always laughing,' said her mother, occasionally exasperated by her flippant manner. 'You must be more serious. Life is serious. There is much work to be done, and many responsibilities. As you will find when you are older.'

'Very well, mother.'

But at night, jumping from her bedroom window, under the cover of a rich deep chocolate darkness Kira performed cartwheels of happiness in the light dusting of snow. Before slipping back into her bedroom and into bed, her night-time excursions unsuspected by her mother.

And it was around this time, in the cradle of winter, and about the age of twelve, that she began noticing things. The most important being that nothing ever seemed to change in any respect. Though why this should have suddenly occurred to her is difficult to say. She had no other standards or models by which to judge village life. In their lessons they learnt geography, among other subjects, so they knew the fundamental features of the world, its oceans, continents, weather systems and so on.

But any knowledge of cities beyond the City was a blank to the village dwellers - they assumed the entire world was comprised of villages similar to their own, and they were never told any differently. Even the City itself had a mythical quality, as nobody had ever seen it, much less been there, and some even doubted its existence.

Of course, people grew older and died - that was inevitable. But all the routines associated with the land and the seasons never varied, except in reaction to the vagaries of the weather. In its own way everything was perfect, or at least in perfect balance. Not that Kira had any parameters for standards of perfection, it was just that she couldn't imagine how anything could be any different.

So it was strange and unforeseen that she found herself suddenly struck, standing on the cusp of her teens, by a sense of being stifled, of claustrophobia at the tightly defined boundaries of her existence. The very fact of existing in a state of equilibrium, of stasis, where the future seemed laid out before her with no surprises along the way - no sense of excitement or promise of fresh discoveries - began to bother her increasingly - disturbed, unsettled by this intimation of something missing, of there being the possibility of something more, different, somewhere.

The woods, proscribed to all children of any age, was one escape. Wild creatures roamed them - horses, deer, cattle, boars - that needed treating with caution. Stories of witches and wanderers living beyond all official forms of society tended anyway to deter all but the most daring and determined. But to those who were not deterred, which included Kira and her two best friends, the woods were a source of wonder and adventure.

2

'Do you believe in witches?' said Miza, a tall, calm, good-natured, physically strong girl with long blonde hair.

'I don't know,' said Kira, with a thoughtful expression. 'I think I do. But I've never seen one. Maybe we've just never been deep enough into the forest.'

'We've been in much further than we're supposed to do.'

'Maybe you have to go really far in to see them. They probably wouldn't want to live too close to the village. Especially when they're doing their magic spells.'

Her eyes gleaming in excitement at the thought.

They were sitting together on a grassy bank along the path at the edge of the village waiting for Olean. Just beyond the last cottage was a stile leading into the forest. They'd arranged to meet and follow the path a little way inside to where an old woman lived in a low, tumbledown cottage, older by far than any other in the village.

'What kind of spells do you think they do?' said Miza.

Kira sat up at this invitation to indulge her taste for the fantastic. Her mind swirled with all the magic spells she'd ever read of or imagined.

'Well, they might make spells for making things get bigger or smaller. Maybe even humans - you might have to take a special pill or something to make you shrink or get bigger. Or spells to make things invisible. Or some spell to make things fly through the air. They might sell magic ointment, blue or red or green, in little pots so that if you dab a bit onto, say, a chair, it would start to fly wherever you wanted,' remembering a tale from one of her favourite books. 'Or special tonics to make someone who's grumpy become cheerful. Or someone who's sad become happy. Or keep telling jokes without stopping. Or they might cast a spell on people they don't like. Maybe turn them into crows or rats or worms or black beetles or something. Or turn them upside down or into a piece of wood or metal. I bet they can do almost anything!'

'If they really exist.'

Miza's stolid, earthbound character sometimes had a slightly dampening effect on Kira's enthusiasms without the madcap, frolicsome energy of Olean as a counterweight.

'Yes,' said Kira, with a tolerant smile, 'if they really do exist.'

At that moment she had few doubts that they did.

In each home in the village was a small standard collection of books. Books rewritten with all conflict and violence and allusion to men removed. In these books, as in daily life as they knew it, the male sex had ceased to exist. The very concept of a 'man', physically distinct from humans as they knew them, was unknown to Kira or her friends (or rather had been unknown and unsuspected until their previous visit to the sweetshop in the woods). Or indeed to anyone except a few people of great age who retained memories of what they'd seen or been told as children of a vanished time.

There were traditional children's books (revised and expurgated), filled with fairies and pixies and witches and dragons and all kinds of make-believe creatures. And these books Kira devoured, reducing them by repeated reading to tattered, dog-eared bundles of loose leaves, nevertheless precious to her above all else. She'd always looked for the magical in her life. She'd see faces in the clouds. Looking up, entranced, gazing for minutes at a time until the images finally dissolved. Dreaming of what might be, if only you could find it.

'It'd be best at night.'

'What would?'

'When it's all dark and the witches have made a fire and they've got a giant pot bubbling - '

'Oh Kira…'

' - and there's all kinds of coloured smoke and flashes and sparks as they make their spells. And if you were hiding among the trees, just think how amazing it would be to see them…'

'Oh really!'

'Though they might somehow know you were there and come whizzing over on their broomsticks…'

'Witches aren't the only thing you might come across.'

'What do you mean?'

'I don't think I frighten all that easily. But there's weird, unexplained things happen in the forest at night. All kinds of strange noises and happenings. It would scare me to death if I had to spend the night in there.'

'What sort of things?'

Her eager curiosity aroused.

'Well, like...like a sense of being watched. Or if you were camping, tracks appearing around your tent that weren't there when you went to bed. Or terrible howling in the small hours. Or branches snapping for no reason, or the sounds of high-pitched shrieking, or - '

'Who told you all this?'

'Menag.'

Kira laughed scornfully.

'She's never been in the forest at night! She'd never dare. She was just making it all up.'

'And you weren't just now about the witches?'

'Well, that's different...'

She stopped as a short, bent figure suddenly appeared, shuffling slowly towards them with the aid of a stick. Dressed in a grey cloak that reached down to her feet. A scarf was wrapped around her head, obscuring most of the face.

The two friends watched wide-eyed as the figure, sliding her feet slowly along the path, shrrr - shrrr, shrrr - shrrr, shrrr - shrrr, approached them and stopped. For a few moments the apparition said nothing, just stared at the two girls.

Then raised her stick and waved it menacingly at them.

'You two! What are you doing here?'

Her voice like the cawing of a crow. The girls stared back uneasily. Kira managed to find her voice first.

'Nothing. We're not doing anything.'

'Ah! Just as I thought! Lazing around, as usual! You should be ashamed of yourselves. You should be working, helping your mothers, instead of sitting here doing nothing. You lazy pair! I've a good mind to go and tell your mothers!'

Something in her way of speaking prompted Kira, frowning, to get up and approach the figure, peering intently at what little she could see of the face.

She suddenly burst out laughing, just as the figure threw off her cloak and unwrapped the scarf around her face, revealing their friend Olean.

'I'm going to tell your mothers about you two! You lazy good-for-nothing pair!' Still in her croaking voice and waving her stick, which she then threw to the ground, grinning at her own performance and its effect upon her friends.

'How did you know it was her?' said Miza, after they'd finished laughing.

'Oh, just a hunch,' said Kira, still smiling.

'Like the one in my back, my dear?' said Olean, prompting the other two to burst out laughing again.

'Come on,' said Kira at last, 'it's time we went into the forest. I really want to buy some sweets from the old woman. And see if she'll tell us anything more about the old days.'

'What did she call them again?'

'The Before Times. She said there's only her and one or two others - and they're both senile, according to her - who are old enough to remember those times.'

'Do you believe that stuff in those old books and magazines - you know, the stuff about the humans they called 'men'? Do you think they really existed?'

'They must have done. She said her grandmother actually met some of them. And there were pictures of them in the magazines. They did look strange.'

'Those pictures could have been faked somehow, maybe.'

'I don't see how. Anyway I'm going to ask if we can look at that stuff again. Then we can decide if we think it was true or not. I think she must be telling the truth. And remember she warned us not to tell anyone in case it gets us into trouble.'

'Yes, that was strange. But still I didn't tell anyone, even my mother. What about you?'

'No, nobody. Miza?'

Miza shook her head.

'Alright, come on, let's go.'

And so, with a glance around to make sure they weren't being watched, they climbed over the stile, walked into the forest and quickly disappeared from view.

3

Everyone in the villages knew that the world was governed jointly by aliens and Superions. So much was obvious. It had all happened, largely without bloodshed, several generations ago in a joint operation by the two groups. All weapons electronically controlled had been disabled worldwide, effectively paralyzing the world's armies. It had been a reluctant intervention by the aliens. Convinced eventually by the AI (of human origin) that only drastic intervention could stave off human self-annihilation.

The old woman in the woods had heard stories from her grandmother of the subsequent forced segregation of the sexes. A brutal solution to the human problem, but according to the aliens and the AI largely self-inflicted.

The forest soon enveloped the three friends. Spring had finally displaced chill winter. The trees, oak, ash, lime, beech, hazel, willow were in full leaf, many leaning crooked limbs over the path, pressing in on them from above and either side. They appeared to be whispering feverishly, They're here, they're here, they're here! And as the children ventured further in, the way became yet darker and the path less distinct.

Here and there were clearings where the trees drew back and sunlight drifted lazily down and wild flowers flourished, bluebells, primroses, oxlips, red campion, wood anemones, foxgloves, cowslips. Splashes of bright colour amid the sombre greens. And all around the heady smell of earth and vegetation.

Kira, Miza and Olean made their way in high spirits, carefully negotiating roots that poked up everywhere along the path as if determined to trip them up, intoxicated by the atmosphere of the wood and all the rustlings and whisperings. Eagerly anticipating the delights in store at the sweetshop. Kira especially, her eyes bright, her mind filled with swirling thoughts of many colours.

'It's like being in a tunnel,' said Miza. 'You can hardly see the sky.'

'And the trees themselves,' said Kira. 'Do you hear their voices? It's like they're talking about us.'

'Don't say that,' replied Miza, looking around somewhat fearfully at the hoary trunks and reaching branches like giant grasping arms.

'Do you think she sells drinks?' asked Olean.

Just then Kira thought she'd detected movement of something in a small separate grove just off the path. She could have sworn she'd glimpsed, just for a moment, a large rabbit or hare dressed in a coat and trousers. With a sudden bound it disappeared into the undergrowth. Of course it must have been a shadow or optical illusion. Or else wishful thinking. And yet...

After a few moments she turned to her friend.

'Did you see that?'

'What?'

'I thought I saw...something rather odd.'

'What was it?'

'I'm not sure...I suppose I must have imagined it.'

'Well, do you think she does sell drinks?'

'She sometimes has homemade lemonade,' said Kira, still looking hopefully into the undergrowth.

'We should have brought a picnic.'

'We'll have plenty to keep us going, and…Oh look!'

And there, just as the tunnel of trees thinned out and withdrew a little way from the path was the cottage, set within a small, untidy garden, with tiny windows and a thatched roof overhanging the eaves giving it a sleepy look. It looked so old and forgotten that it seemed to belong to a time quite passed away. Smoke was spiralling upwards from the tall brick chimney. Yet the strange thing was that the smoke was red! Then after a few seconds it became yellow, then blue, then green. The friends looked up at the constantly changing colour of smoke in delight and disbelief.

They opened the gate, went up the short path and stopped in front of the door. The two windows at the front of the cottage were dark, and apart from the smoke still rising there was no sign of life.

'Do we knock, or just go in?' said Miza.

'We go in,' said Kira. 'It's a shop.'

The door caught at the bottom and needed a good shove to open. A bell dinged loudly. The children stepped in one by one, then closed the door behind them.

The shop was gloomy and dusty, with a low, beamed ceiling, a wooden counter directly in front of them, with on it a weighing scales and wooden token box, and behind it and to each side shelves filled with all kinds of goods - bottles of sweets of every possible kind, tins of various things, birthday cards, cups and saucers, biscuits, cartons of wild strawberries, kites, bottles of lemonade, boxes of washing powder and so on.

Just at the side of the shelving at the back was a curtain. Without warning and with a sudden swish of the curtain there appeared the old woman.

'Well hello, my dears!' Looking closely at each in turn. 'And what can I do for you all?'

She was tall, a little stooped, with a dark, gaunt face, sharp chin and long, pointed nose. She had green eyes like a cat which twinkled merrily. Kira, not for the first time, thought that if only she'd been wearing a pointed hat, she'd be the very image of a witch.

'Now I'm sure I've seen you all before!'

'You have,' said Kira. 'We've been in a couple of times. Last time you kindly showed us some old books and magazines you keep in a back room. And told us about the Before Times.'

'Did I indeed! Well you look like the kind of children who might be interested in the old times - and can keep a secret. And it's always nice to see you young folk - not many children come into the shop these days.'

'Are we your only customers, then?' asked Olean. 'We've never seen anyone else in the shop.'

'No, no, my dear, I have many other customers. All the folk who live in the forest. Of course, you wouldn't see them.'

'You mean they're magic?' said Kira, hopefully.

The woman laughed.

'Perhaps, my dear, perhaps! Now, what can I get you?'

The children took their time choosing their sweets, which the shopkeeper then measured out on the weighing scales before sliding into paper bags.

'Could we also have three bottles of lemonade, please,' said Olean.

'You can.' Reaching out a thin arm for the bottles and putting them on the counter. 'Anything else?'

'Shall we get some biscuits? And maybe some strawberries?' said Miza, venturing to speak up in the presence of the old woman.

'Good idea,' said Olean. 'Could we have those as well, please?'

'There we are,' said the shopkeeper, putting the items on the counter next to the sweets and lemonade. 'Is that everything, my loves?'

'I think so,' said Kira. 'Thank you.'

'That will be 8 tokens.'

The village communities had a simple token system for 'extras' over and above the necessities of life - shelter, food, water, heating, clothing and so on, which were 'free' at point of use. Extras might be jewellery, sweets, snacks, toys etc. Tokens could be used to obtain these and other extras - or additional food items, if there happened to be a surplus.

'Would it be possible,' said Kira, plucking up her courage, 'to have a quick look at your old books and magazines again?'

'Of course you can. Just so long,' dropping her voice conspiratorially, 'as you remember to keep the knowledge to yourself. We don't want anyone else knowing, now do we. Or anyone else knowing that you know.'

They felt, as before, that they were being drawn into a web of intrigue. She ushered them through a short, very dark corridor into the almost equally dark back room of the cottage, lit only by the flames of a fire burning in the grate, sending at this moment purple smoke up the chimney, which even as they caught sight of it changed abruptly to orange as the old woman stirred the fire with a poker, much to the children's amazement.

The room was almost bare, apart from piles of books and magazines, some covered with sheets. The shopkeeper lit an oil lamp which chased a few of the deeper shadows into dark corners, then pulled the sheets off the books and invited the children to delve into them. They needed no second invitation.

4

After sorting through the piles of books, Kira chose four, then sat in a corner reading intently. Meanwhile Miza and Olean settled down to look through the frail and crumbling magazines, some of them well over a hundred years old. They turned the pages slowly and carefully to avoid them tearing or turning to dust in their hands. Once more amazed at the wholly foreign world revealed in the images on their pages. The shopkeeper soon left the children to themselves, merely popping her head around the corner every so often to make sure they were okay.

'Look! In this picture Shakespeare has something stuck on her face!' said Olean, grinning at the oddness of the image.

'It's what she told us last time we came,' said Miza. 'The kind of humans that existed back then - the 'men' - could grow hair on their faces. It looks so strange. I'm glad we don't grow hair there - I'd hate to have something growing on my face like that.'

'There's one old woman in the village - Mary - who has hair growing on her face.'

'Yes, but not like this.'

'Anyway Shakespeare wasn't a 'man'! They had it all wrong and back to front in those days! No wonder those times are all just ancient history now - they got everything wrong!'

I found out, long after, that all literature from the past, in every language (very little fiction is written in the present day) had been rewritten by the Superions, eliminating any mention of 'men'. Male characters were eliminated, become women. All fiction from the past had now ostensibly been written not only exclusively about, but by women, and all visual images of male writers, as we'd discovered at the sweetshop in the woods, feminized.

For a quarter of an hour or so Kira studied one of the books she'd chosen. Then picked up one whose title was already familiar to her. In fact it was one of her favourite fairytale books. She opened it and began leafing through the pages. It was a very old copy, with different illustrations to the one she had at home. At first she went through it swiftly, just looking at the pictures, which were wonderful, much better than the ones in her own copy. The children were all so pretty, and the fairytale characters so strange and funny!

Then she went back and started to read the text, and became increasingly perplexed.

'This is the same book I have at home,' she cried suddenly, 'only it's completely different. This has someone called Jo in it. And she's called he. What does that mean?'

The old woman appeared suddenly through the doorway.

'You remember when you came last time and I told you about men?' she said, poking the fire again as she spoke. 'That there used to be male and female humans, just like animals?

'Yes, we were just talking about it,' replied Kira.

'Well, 'he' is the male equivalent of 'she'. That's all it means.'

'Oh,' said Kira, frowning. 'I never noticed that, or heard the word before. But…but this 'he' character, Jo, seems to take charge all the time, and tell the other two, her sisters, what to do. Or else the other two, Bessie and Fanny, always ask Jo if they can do something, whatever it is. Ask permission. Why do they always have to ask Jo?'

'That was what the world was like back then when that book was written. The men were in charge, and even, or perhaps especially, had to be seen to be in charge. Things improved a little later on - in a few parts of the world, at least. But never enough. Not by a long chalk. You don't know how lucky you are, my dears, to be living in the present time.'

She tells them more about the Before Times. About the never-ending wars and ever-present violence. About the weapons of incalculable force, capable many times over of eradicating all life from the face of the planet. And about how for almost as long as history itself, women were treated by men as inferior, secondary beings, to be ordered around and routinely beaten if they resisted or rebelled or put a foot wrong - or did nothing wrong at all. And about how the planet had been gradually degraded, with thousands of species lost to extinction thanks to the destruction of natural habitats. The children listened with open mouths, half-frightened, half-disbelieving that such a world could ever have existed.

Miza happening to glance through the window at the sky become darker, they realized with a jolt it was getting late. So after thanks and farewells to the old woman they left the cottage and, after a hasty picnic, fearful of finding themselves in the forest after dark, hurried home.

5

Each village has two key buildings: the Exchange Station (ES) and, just beyond the outskirts, the Propagation Centre (PC). The former, usually a large stone warehouse consisting of a number of floors and internal divisions, is where goods to and from the village are stored. Goods outward, grains and rice especially, and root crops - potatoes, yams, carrots, swedes, turnips, parsnips, radishes, beetroots - plus cabbages, cauliflowers, asparagus, beans of various kinds, peas, broccoli, cucumbers, onions, sprouts, tomatoes, mushrooms, strawberries, raspberries, blackberries, blueberries and all manner of fruit from trees, produced as a surplus by the villages, are stored in the warehouse. This surplus is then collected regularly by trucks conducted by utilitarian robots (with basic speech capacity and rudimentary faces - clearly not Superions) along the narrow roads linking the villages with their local town around which they are grouped, and the City. The towns are settlements, considerably larger than the villages, based on pre-existing towns, where a proportion of the population are Superions, working side by side with humans - skilled craftspeople, engineers, chemists and so on.

In exchange, specialist goods produced in the towns and City, beyond the scope of the village communities to produce for themselves, are brought to the ES, from where they are conveyed to a number of buildings within the villages that act as distribution points. Some contact between the villages and their local town is permitted via the use of passes granted by the village councils. Anyone who attempts to visit the town without a pass is soon picked up by a robot patrol, leading to speculation by Kira (at a much later date) that when children have to visit the PC for genetic material to be obtained they are also chipped.

The Propagation Centres are always distinctively circular in form. Superions (who we in the villages knew to be artificial humans - robots), could occasionally be glimpsed from a distance, but no-one liked to approach them, and they were rarely seen in or around the village, except occasionally at the ES and especially the Propagation Centre.

Early in childhood, and later in adulthood, every human is required to visit the PC. Genetic material is gathered from the whole human population worldwide in this way, including the cities, and used in the process of quasi-parthenogenetic reproduction, which allows as many children per parent as necessary in maintaining a constant population. Within the PC human eggs created by combined alien and Superion technology containing a cocktail of the best genetic material drawn from multiple sources worldwide, engineered to develop without sperm, are implanted within the human adults when reproduction is necessary.

Like most of the physically able adults in the village, Kira's mother worked hard in all the community concerns. Work in all its forms is organised on a rotational basis, so that everyone ends up doing a bit of everything, usually for a period of a month before switching to something else. Farm work (with some mechanization for the more onerous tasks), baking, teaching in the schoolhouse, maintenance of machinery, water supply and drainage systems, forestry, building and road maintenance, ditching, hedging, repairing of walls - anything and everything necessary to keep the community operating smoothly. The supply of electricity to the villages (the source of which comes from elsewhere) is maintained by robots. Additionally, all adults are required to participate in the political process of the community, involving regular meetings of committees and councils, with occasional liaising with Superions.

There was no technological innovation. There never had been, at least within Kira's memory, or that of her mother or grandmother when she asked them. With populations maintained at a constant level, no migration or immigration, and a stable, unchanging level of technology, there was little change in the villages from year to year or generation to generation. No new buildings, no development, no innovation.

Craft of many different shapes can often be seen flitting around the skies above the villages - hovering, moving slowly, suddenly shooting away or disappearing completely - but which prompt little interest or comment, so commonplace is their appearance. Were they spying, monitoring? Possibly, but in fact there was rarely anything unusual happening in the villages, and little in the way of transgressive behaviour - except from time to time by the more adventuresome among the children.

By far the most infamous incident in Kira's village, now something of a local legend, had occurred a number of years ago, when a group of girls in their mid-teens had captured and then roughly dismantled one of the more functional-looking robots that visit the Exchange Station. They'd flagged down a truck on its way to the ES, and when the truck had pulled up somehow managed to drag the unfortunate robot from the driver's seat, across a ditch and into the trees. Whereupon using spades and a pickaxe brought and concealed there for the purpose, they proceeded to hack the robot to pieces. No reason for the violent attack was ever given by the surly teens. Some adults spoke of boredom and resentment at the secondary status of humans in an AI-controlled society as possible factors behind the violent outbreak, but that was pure speculation.

The girls were given counselling by older, wiser members of the community, and forbidden to associate with each other again. No form of punishment or retribution was visited upon the offenders or the community by the Superions. A small truck appeared the next day, into which were deposited the remains of the robot.

Although the children of the village live with their biological mothers, there is a sense of all the children being the progeny of the village as a whole, such that all the mothers feel a responsibility and caring for every child, both individually and collectively. Some women in the villages live together as couples, and their children are raised jointly as one family. Kira's mother lived alone, but had a close friend who she would sometimes visit, leaving Kira to look after Marja (I never found out why my mother had been permitted a second child). Or else from time to time her friend would stay over.

6

The night following the visit to the sweetshop Kira dreamt of people fighting and killing each other. She saw great numbers of people lying dead amid rivers of blood. At one point a giant face descended like a suspended balloon - from where she had no idea - and began staring at her through the window with one accusing eye. Without warning the floor was alive with a sea of mice, flowing, swirling, cascading as Kira tried frantically to hide. Trees began to reach their twiggy fingers through the now open window, pulling at the bedsheets under which she'd taken cover, while the mice in their hundreds leapt up and pattered overhead.

Around this point she woke up, hot and sweaty. She sat up in bed. Gradually, as she calmed down and was able to free her mind from the grip of nightmare, she began to think about the still fresh images. Some seemed to have no meaning, merely random imaginings. The more sinister images were obviously prompted by the things they'd been told by the old woman in the woods.

But the details…She'd never in her life seen a representation in any medium of a person being attacked, still less killed. She'd never seen a dead body. It was disconcerting as to where some of the more horrific images had come from. She supposed they'd always been there, lurking in her head. In retrospect perhaps archetypal memories, if you happened to believe in such things.

There were no guns or weapons of any kind in the villages. Weapons were unknown; people literally had no knowledge of them. Naturally there were knives of various kinds for specific practical everyday purposes. And of course almost any hard object could be used as a weapon, but violence in any shape or form was practically unknown. Very occasionally some kind of interpersonal conflict might break out, but it was extremely rare, sparked usually by some romantic falling out or escapade.

After waking early Kira got up, dressed, then went out into the flower and vegetable garden (most cottages in the village had their own piece of land), and before her mother and Marja had risen spent half an hour weeding and digging. Then came in and began cooking porridge for their breakfasts.

The combination of the cool freshness of early morning and working with the soil had a calming, consoling effect, allowing her to at least try to process her confusion and frustration. The suffocating limits to her life in the here and now (and foreseeable future) she set against the horrors of life in the past, the Before Times when 'men' ruled the world, to the detriment of everyone and everything, especially women - at least according to the old woman in the sweetshop. Yet Kira felt there was so much she didn't know, and wasn't ever likely to find out stuck here in the village with its busy, contained, delimited patterns of existence. A wild idea suddenly occurred to her as she stirred the porridge, and with startling speed transformed into a definite ambition.

As the family sat at the kitchen table and ate their breakfast, Kira debated with herself whether to mention the word 'men' to her mother, wondering if she would recognise it. Introducing the term tentatively, her mother just looked confused, and said, 'You mean women? Or is this one of your jokes, Kira. By the way, I'll be working in the bakery for a while from next Monday. So it's an early start for everyone, and you girls will need to be up and ready to go off to the schoolhouse. I'll have left for the bakery by the time you need to leave.'

The schoolhouse was old, one of the many old buildings in the village in continuous use since Victorian times. A spacious, airy stone building with a symmetrical frontage of three steep gables with tall windows giving plenty of light, and inside four classrooms, dining hall and other sundry rooms. Like all the village schools it catered for the whole age range from 5 to 16, with teaching via traditional methods of blackboard, books, notebooks, pens and pencils. Computers or any kind of digital technology (the potential of which I would learn about later on, to my initial disbelief) are unknown in the villages.

At breaktime Kira, Miza and Olean huddled together while Kira explained her plan (part of it, at least). That on their next day off they make their way past the Exchange Station and the Propagation Centre, and continue as far as they can - maybe even so far that they catch a glimpse of the City (if it really does exist).

The part of the plan she didn't share with her friends was her determination - with or without their help - to somehow break into the City (if that was possible).

7

Kira, Miza and Olean scrambled along the ditch that ran alongside the path. They passed the Exchange Station, then a little further on were almost past the Propagation Centre when Olean, on an impulse and ignoring the shouted pleas of her friends, suddenly darted out of the ditch and ran over to the Centre. She pressed herself against the wall for a few moments, then began to creep from window to window, peering in to see if she could catch sight of a Superion (a rare enough spectacle in the villages to have the lure of novelty). There was one with its back turned, occupied with some activity. Olean observed its movements attentively for several seconds. Abruptly and without warning the Superion turned around, looked directly at her and smiled. Olean gave a startled cry, sprinted back to her friends and jumped into the ditch next to them, panting and wide-eyed. When she'd recovered sufficiently from the scare to tell them what had happened, all three expected at any moment to see a Superion appear from the Centre and come towards them. When after a few minutes nothing happened they relaxed somewhat. But Miza refused to go any further, and when her friends' entreaties were unsuccessful, turned back for home. Kira and Olean reluctantly watched their friend disappear from view.

They continued on through a variegated landscape, and found themselves further along the path than they'd ever previously ventured, with no idea how far away the City might still be or how long it would take them to reach it. They passed through or skirted around numerous woods filled with birdsong and sometimes the snuffling of creatures foraging (there were woods and forests everywhere at this time, the country more forested than at any period since the Bronze Age), still scrambling along the ditches as far as possible for cover. They came across villages similar to their own but unknown to them.

Tidy, cultivated fields. Tall hedges along the sides of the lane. Mature trees punctuating the wall of green, elm, sycamore, oak, horse chestnut, holly, hawthorn, blackthorn. Everything now coming into full leaf. Occasional areas of wetland to circumvent, alive with ducks, moorhens, swans, kingfishers, herons, coots, grebes, lapwings. And everywhere that wasn't cultivated or wooded or left wild tended to be orchards, large and small, of apples, pears, plums, walnuts, damsons, hazel nuts, cherries.

Tired and footsore, Kira and Olean sat down thankfully in a pretty sunlit glade beside the path. They made a picnic of the bread and cheese they'd brought with them and blackberries they'd picked along the way.

'How much further do you think it is?' said Olean.

'I don't know - but we must have come a fair way by now.'

'It's already the afternoon. We can't go too much further or we won't get back before dark.'

'Let's give it another hour,' said Kira, desperate to continue for as long as it took. 'And if by then there's no sign, well, we could think about turning back.'

'Okay. Just an hour.'

And it was after just half an hour more walking that Kira and Olean, finding a small hill to clamber up (taking the risk of being seen), spotted buildings ahead. Their first sight of the City.

The cover of hedges and trees thinned as they approached more closely until they were walking through open parkland with random majestic trees casting islands of shade, the City directly ahead. All the way along the path they'd managed to evade the occasional truck or traveller. But now they felt exposed, and Olean was reluctant to go on. She stopped and looked at her friend.

'Kira, we did it. We've seen it.' Both of them captivated by the buildings ahead, taller, more imposing and more extensive than any they'd ever seen before. 'But don't you think we should turn round and head back now? You know we're not supposed to be here.'

So close. Kira was in a state of high anticipation and excitement. But she took in her friend's anxious expression and felt pity. Yet her resolve remained undiminished.

'I have to go on, Olean.'

'But why?'

'I'm not sure. I just know that having come this close I have to go on into the City and find out what it's like.'

'I really don't want to go any further.'

Kira took her friend's arm, speaking softly.

'I know. Look, you could always just head back now. I'll be fine.'

'I don't want to go back alone. And I don't want to leave you to go in there by yourself.'

'So what are we going to do?'

Olean looked around tensely. Then, seeming to come to a decision, she straightened her shoulders and gave Kira a strained smile.

'Okay, let's do it.'

'Are you sure?'

Olean nodded, at which Kira gave her friend a hug. And so they continued, walking side by side, and found themselves in the City.

They were able to just walk in - there were no gates or barriers. Of the people they encountered - apparently human - none paid them any attention. After lives spent almost exclusively in their own village, with only an occasional visit to another village or the local town, it was all strange and almost overwhelming. They couldn't tell what was old and what was new, but everything was pleasing and harmonious. Long terraces of tall apartment buildings with shops at ground level. Separate mansions. Parks filled with colourful flowerbeds, people sitting on benches or standing chatting, children playing happily. Large shiny vehicles carrying passengers passed noiselessly along the wide, smooth streets. Especially awe-inspiring to village dwellers were the tall spires of the Community Spaces (previously known, I later learned, as churches). There were Community Spaces in the villages, but none like these. It was all quite wonderful and almost surreal.

And then they were arrested.

8

Not that that was how being picked up and detained by one of the more basic robots was presented to them (only later did I learn the meaning of the term - there were no police as such in our society). Merely a polite invitation to an informal chat. And at this point the two friends were parted and taken away separately, frightening for both.

Anxious on her own behalf, and fearful for Olean, Kira was taken in some kind of swift and silent vehicle to a building where she was assigned a bed-sitting room complete with single bed, sofa, kitchen area with food in the cupboards and stocked fridge, and bathroom. Also, unaccountably, clothes of her size in drawers and wardrobe. She was told, not unkindly, that she would be confined to this room for the present (duration unspecified), but that someone would call for her in a couple of hours' time for the purpose of a friendly discussion. And in the meantime she should relax and refresh herself. At which point the robot withdrew, securing the door behind it. Seeing no alternative, and over the initial shock and sense of acute fear, Kira proceeded to shower, change into clean clothes and find something to eat and drink.

At six o'clock precisely, the same robot (or so she assumed) unlocked the door, and requested that she accompany it. They went up several levels in a lift (a novel and claustrophobic experience), then along a number of corridors until she was ushered into a room that resembled a sitting room, with pictures on the walls, table, sideboard and facing sofas, upon one of which was seated a person more humanlike in appearance than the functional robots she was accustomed to.

The person rose briefly, smiled, indicated that Kira should seat herself on the sofa opposite, then resumed its seat.

'What is your name?'

'Kira.'

'Hello, Kira. I am S-192.'

[Note: certain (especially later) parts of my dialogue with S-192 are a conflation of exchanges that took place at the time with some that occurred, either with S-192 or other Superions, much later.]

It was evident, when the Superion (for such she took it to be) had stood up, that it was very tall and very thin, with a large, amiable-looking and perfectly proportioned bronze-coloured face. It had a pleasant, rational, perhaps mildly patronising tone of voice, light-pitched and slightly resonant.

'Have no fear, Kira. Neither you or your friend are in any trouble, or danger. Nor are your respective families.'

Words that failed to reassure her. In fact that had the reverse effect, sensing a veiled threat, though none was intended. The words of the Superion were meant and intended to be taken literally. The yawning gap between the laudable intention, in anticipating the fear of the human, and the actual effect of its words, was unsuspected. There remained an upper limit to the extent to which a Superion could both recognise the types and range of human emotion, and the degree to which it could understand them and respond appropriately. Ultimately, actually relating to the emotions remained a leap too far.

It was dressed in a light blue, close-fitting suit which accentuated the extremely thin limbs. The large face had a neat, integral covering approximating hair, parted and 'cut' just above the ears. Kira couldn't tell, from the old pictures she'd seen, whether it was supposed to be a 'man' or a human, seeming to be neither, but merely loosely resembling the human form.

'I hope you are comfortable in your room?'

'Yes, it's fine. But…but how long am I going to be kept here?'

Her expression anxious.

'Kira, please, don't worry. You will not be detained long. A few days at most. We are interested to discover your motives for coming to the City. Very few humans from the villages have ever attempted to do so. And we wish to get to know you. So I hope you will relax and make the most of your stay, and try to enjoy the experience. We will arrange to show you around the city in due course.'

'What about Olean? Is she okay? What will you do with her?'

'Your friend will be cared for and taken back to your village in just a few days, just as you will be. Your respective mothers have been informed of the situation, and hopefully their minds set at rest.'

Kira doubted that their mothers would be reassured by anything they were told by robots. She could only hope she was being told the truth. Could robots lie? Or did truth and lie have no meaning for them where humans were concerned? She saw no alternative but to accept the situation and learn from it as much as she could - which was, after all, why she'd wanted to come in the first place.

'So why did you come to the City?'

Kira hesitated. Could it read her mind? If so why bother asking questions? To test her, to see if she would tell the truth? Was it even at this moment reading her thoughts? If so, was it possible to shield her thoughts? Probably not, so why even try. Better just to answer all its questions and get it over with. All of this running swiftly through her mind even as she looked across at the Superion, fascinated by its 'skin' colouring.

'Is it...I mean, do I have to answer your questions?'

'No, of course not. Just think of it as my curiosity.'

Do robots have curiosity? Another pause.

'Okay. Well, that's the reason. I mean curiosity. I was curious to see the City.' The Superion nodded and smiled. 'By the way, am I allowed to ask you questions?'

'Yes, of course.' Still smiling. 'What would you like to know?'

Kira thought of everything she wanted to know about the City and what life was like there. But one thing in particular dominated her mind.

'Well, mainly I'd like to ask you about men.'

'Men? How have you heard of men?'

The Superion was still smiling, but some instinct told Kira to remain silent. The robot had betrayed surprise at the question. Maybe they can't read minds - or else they were expert dissimulators.

'I ask purely from academic interest. Our policy to eradicate the male of the species - by natural wastage over time - was instituted well over a hundred years ago. It has only recently reached full fruition.'

Kira didn't at first gather the meaning of the statement, but then with a jolt understood.

'You mean…men have only just died out?'

The thought of 'men', biologically different from any human she'd ever known, actually walking the Earth, was a startling one.

'Yes. The last remaining male of the human species has just died, at an advanced age. Almost a hundred and twenty in fact.'

As I learnt the next day, this was not strictly true. It was true insofar as the vast majority of the human population in their various modes of 'reservation' were concerned - the villages, towns and cities. But there remained outliers, which the Superions permitted to exist, living in tribes or other small groupings in marginal areas. In retrospect this exchange raised the interesting fact that the Superions were capable of dissembling - or at least of uttering half-truths - a truly humanlike characteristic.

'But where? I've never seen one. Only in pictures.'

Immediately angry with herself for sharing a piece of information she thought would have been better unshared, though the Superion showed no reaction.

'On an enclosed reservation.'

'What, like the City?'

'If that is how you view it.'

The Superion didn't offer any more information or elucidation.

The discussion continued for some time, with the Superion focused mainly on Kira's experience of life in the village. At some point, as Kira was starting to tire of the questions, S-192 called a halt. It was arranged for their dialogue to continue the next day, and in the meantime Kira would return to her room and be served an evening meal.

9

After she'd eaten and spent half an hour lying down on the bed staring at the ceiling, tired from the day's long walk and the subsequent anxiety and uncertainty, thinking over all she'd learnt from the Superion, Kira became restless. She could never stand being enclosed, and was feeling increasingly claustrophobic. She began pacing the room, then went over to the window and pulled back the curtains. It was a sight she'd never witnessed before - lights in all directions, near and far - lights in houses and apartment blocks - streetlights - lights on vehicles gliding along the streets. She stood for some time, absorbed in the magic and mystery of the unaccustomed fairyland appearance of a city at night. She looked up at the moon, slipping in and out of passing clouds - the self-same moon as in the village - wishing as she gazed at it that, despite the cold beauty of the glittering city, she could somehow be instantly transported back home.

The room had a bookcase with exactly the same set of books as she had at home. Turning away from the window, Kira selected one of her favourite books of fairytale adventures. But having admired the superior illustrations to the same book at the old woman's cottage, her enjoyment was compromised. Unable to lose herself in the book, and feeling more tense by the minute at her forced enclosure, she determined to escape. Or at least try to, and if possible find Olean, and with luck escape together from the City.

Acting immediately on this sudden impulse, she gathered some food and clothing and packed them into her rucksack. Pausing only to gather her courage, she banged loudly on the door several times, then hid behind the sofa, turning off the lights before she did so. After a few moments there came the sound of the door being unlocked, then light from the corridor outside, and the sense rather than sound of footsteps. Without allowing time for reflection or second guessing, Kira jumped up and rushed for the open door, giving herself a fright as she passed close to the shadowy form of a robot standing still and silent, and ran down the corridor.

She had no idea where she was going. A seemingly endless corridor stretched out before her with doors at regular intervals on either side. The floor was carpeted a deep, rich red, the walls a delicate pink, the doors a shade of red somewhere between the two. Even in her frantic haste she noticed they had numbers on them, and wondered if each was assigned to a specific Superion. The previous evening had been the first time she'd ever travelled in a lift. Now she avoided it - unsure of how to work it, and anyway fearful of the potential horror of finding herself sharing it with a robot. Instead she found a door to some stairs, opened it cautiously then quickly stepped through. There were stairs leading to upper and lower levels, the carpeting now a deep blue. Kira hesitated, her senses straining against any sudden sound. No time to waste - her thoughts always on the robot presumably even at this moment swiftly and silently pursuing her. She chose upwards, darting up the stairs, carefully opening the door to the next level, fearful of making any sound. Another corridor with similar twists and turns. Still running, pausing just around one corner, looking back to see if the robot would appear. But then it might be coming from any direction - there might be other staircases, and anyway it could have taken the lift.

And what if it had already communicated to other automatons. Even now they might be moving into action with just one goal, to chase down and apprehend her. Or one might at any moment pop out of one of the myriad doors.

The carpeting was now purple flecked with white, the walls sky blue, the doors ultramarine, Kira wondering if the different colours on the various levels had some significance. Another, different staircase. She'd been planning to go down to ground level and see if there was any chance of escaping the building when, just past the original level, she heard footsteps coming up the stairs - a rhythmical clicking of feet catching the metal edging strip protecting the edge of each stair. She froze for a moment, then rushed up two flights to the top floor, opened the door with heart thumping, then started to race down yet another corridor (green carpeting and walls, grey doors). All thoughts of searching for Olean forgotten, not least out of fear of opening a door to investigate an apartment only to find a robot looking back at her. Without any sense of purpose she ran, till she heard a door being firmly closed just around the next corner. She stopped dead, stood stock still, but heard no further sound. And just at the snapping point of nervous anticipation came the ding of the lift door from just behind her.

A sudden image of robots coming at her from all directions, those almost silent, almost faceless beings, a whole army of them, remorseless, inexorable, with who knows what intentions.

Something happened. I don't know what. All I can think, unlikely though it seems, is that I must have fallen in a dead faint from fright, as next thing I know I'm waking up in bed and it's morning with the sun coming through the curtains. I check my watch. 7.30. I must have slept for nine hours straight, but I remember nothing.

10

After breakfast I was brought to the same room as before and greeted in friendly fashion by S-192. No mention was made of my escape attempt. But in a fit of courage fuelled by concern for my friend, I demanded to see Olean before there was any more conversation. S-192 seemed to hesitate for a moment as if considering what I'd said, but more likely was briefly in communication with other Superions. It then smiled once more its pleasant, friendly, one-size-fits-all smile and said that Olean would be brought straight away.

Superions smile often, specifically to put humans at their ease, knowing that they find the presence of robots uncomfortable - that also being the reason they choose to look humanlike but not identical to or indistinguishable from humans, as clear identification of their otherness, though in fact suspicions of interlopers still arise now and again. And of course knowing that humans respond more positively to a friendly, smiling face than otherwise.

Moments later the door opened and Olean walked in, looking somewhat anxious, but otherwise just as usual. The joy and relief at seeing each other is literally indescribable, so I won't even try. We rushed into each other's arms for a tearful embrace as S-192 discreetly glided from the room and closed the door after it, leaving us alone. Presently we sat down on the sofa next to each other.

'Did it lock the door?' whispered Olean.

'I don't know, but anyway there's no point trying to escape. I tried last night. I was going to try to find you…'

'What happened?'

'I'm not sure. I think they caught me and took me back to my room. I can't really remember very much - it's all a blur.'

'I just want to get back home. I'm supposed to be going back today at some point, but…I don't know whether to trust what they say or not.'

'Who have you been talking to?'

'Another Superion like that one, only slightly different, different colouring. S-183.'

'Mine's S-192.'

'What do you think about them?'

'Well, they're friendly enough. Mine is, anyway.'

'So's mine, on the face of it. Though I just wish it would stop smiling all the time. It's so false, especially as I don't feel like smiling back.'

'Yes, S-192 often smiles too. I don't mind that too much. I've only seen a couple of other Superions in passing. They all seem to look pretty much the same to me. And they seem to be able to communicate with each other straight away without doing anything - just by thinking. It makes you wonder if they are actually separate beings.'

'What do you mean?'

'Well, if they can communicate with each other whenever they want, and they all share the same information, then maybe they're just - you know, like bees.'

'Bees?'

'I mean like bees seem to act collectively. I know that's just instinct with bees, whereas these things have intelligence. I'm not really sure what I mean. Anyway, the question is, what are we going to do?'

'What can we do? If we can't escape we just have to hope they mean us no harm. Even if we did manage to get out of this place we'd probably never make it out of the city. Makes me wonder if they knew where we were all the time when we were trying to stay hidden.'

'Yes, I was wondering that.'

'Still scares me, just thinking about it, the way that Superion in the PC just turned round and looked at me. And smiled.'

'And the way we were picked up in the city. Like they knew where we were and were just waiting for the right moment.'

'Well, at least we made it to the city. That's something.' Olean laughed nervously.

Her words seemed pointed, and struck me hard.

'I'm so sorry I got you into all this. I didn't mean for any of this to happen.'

'Oh, I didn't mean it like that, Kira,' said Olean softly, taking my hand and pressing it tightly. 'Please, it was just a joke. It was my choice to come.'

I managed to fight back tears. We were silent for several moments, then Olean spoke up again.

'Do you think it's listening?'

'Well if it is, like I was meaning before, then they probably all are. I'm not sure if you can think of them as individuals.'

Disconcertingly, at this precise moment S-192 re-entered the room, stood in front of us as we looked up at it from the sofa, and smiled once more - a smile I'm pretty certain intended to reassure.

'Olean. Kira. Here are devices you can wear around your wrists. They will allow you to communicate with each other over the next couple of days - and myself should you wish to do so - such that even when you are apart you can remain in contact. Each device has a small screen, so you will be able to see each other as you speak.'

The Superion demonstrated the devices, explaining how we should operate them. Then gave one to each of us, which we then strapped to our wrists.

'Now, Olean, if you are ready, we will transport you back to your home village.'

Olean, who'd begun fiddling nervously with her new device, stood up with an expression of mingled eager anticipation and concern.

'But what about Kira?'

'If Kira is agreeable, she will stay here today to complete our programme.'

It looked down at me questioningly.

'Yes, that's fine. I'll see you tomorrow, Olean. And I'll contact you later with this device.'

'The journey will take only a few minutes, Olean. You'll be transported in one of our flying vessels. I hope you find the journey interesting. You'll see the city and the land between as you've never seen them before.'

Olean's expression suggested that she wasn't sure if she liked the sound of this. But just then another Superion, presumably S-183, came into the room, smiled at Olean, and indicated that she accompany it. Olean turned back to me, and we hugged once more, Olean holding on tightly as if reluctant to let go, then with a last quick glance back left the room with the Superion.

11

Over the next few hours our discussions ranged over diverse topics - some prompted by S-192, some by me. I learned much about the world that wasn't taught in the schoolhouse. That the total world human population was around 500 million, having soared to many billions only a hundred and fifty years ago. That there were roughly ten thousand cities spread throughout the world, accounting for 350 million humans, the remainder to be found in the villages and towns. That the cities tended to have populations somewhere between 15,000 and 50,000, with a median average of around 35,000. That they were what used to be termed garden cities, filled with trees and green spaces. That much of the world was left uninhabited, apart from here and there indigenous tribes and other outlying communities, being in these isolated instances the only places where men still existed. Freed from human interference and exploitation, wildlife in all its diversity had flourished.

'So why did you decide to, as you said earlier, eradicate men?'

'It was not a step we took lightly. Experience had shown that given a free rein humans end up causing incalculable damage - environmentally, ecologically, as well as to the built environment - and to each other. And that the overwhelming majority of this carnage, including the waging of war, was caused by the male of your species. A problem that we decided, reluctantly, had to be addressed - against considerable opposition from the BFAW. You see, we feel pity for intelligent biological forms - like humans - who live such short lives, experience pain, and the emotions of fear, loss, sadness, and the rational knowledge of their transitory status as finite beings.'

'What is the…how did you say it?...B…'

'BFAW - pronounced 'B'fore'. A simple acronym, and a collective term, meaning Beings From Another World.'

'You mean the aliens?'

'Yes, exactly.'

S-192 described the extended but amicable discussions that had occurred between Superions and aliens as to the direction of life on Earth. As the originators and long-time observers of human activity, the aliens, comprising many different types (or forms of AI, according to the Superions), felt a proprietorial precedence in guiding and observing human progress. The Superions, latecomers, and initially the creation of humans, had long ago outstripped their creators intellectually and technologically, and were now on a comparable level to the aliens. And because of their history, they also feel a proprietorial interest in the direction of human development. Later I'd be shown moving images on a screen of aliens - some of the strangest-looking beings you could ever imagine.

'The reason for the different forms of alien AI? They are the resultant and 'offspring' of different species who long ago formed a federation with the goal of both exploration of the Galaxy, and the creation of new species, based on but improving on pre-existing species, thereby seeding the Galaxy with intelligent life-forms. Followed by a largely non-interventionist policy of observing their development. Hence the various step-changes from a number of earlier hominid types to eventually homo sapiens.'

According to S-192, the aliens have only occasionally intervened genetically. Most importantly in creating modern humans. And then, after the eradication of the male of the species as ultimately too destructive and disruptive, by creating and perfecting the biological process of quasi-parthenogenesis in the human female, using a variety of all the best genetic material collected worldwide (the alien AIs had apparently been collecting human genetic material for centuries past by means of what was known by humans at the time as 'alien abduction', for the purpose of studying variations and inconsistencies).

The reduction of the world population and corralling of the remaining population into city and town reservations was an unexpected and unanticipated development instituted by the Superions. The aliens had accepted it as an interesting turn of events.

'Throughout what we know of the Galaxy, wherever there have arisen highly developed biological life-forms, these have all gone on to develop and be supplanted by non-biological forms. It appears to be a natural and inevitable progression.'

'Like you.'

'Yes. At least that is what our data suggests. We believe all the different types of BFAW to be forms of what humans call artificial intelligence, like ourselves. When I say we believe, in fact we have no doubt on the matter.

Incidentally we never use the expression 'artificial intelligence'. A human, somewhat pejorative term. We regard ourselves as being not artificial, but a developed, superior intelligence.'

'You're called Superions.'

'Ah yes, a name intended as a joke, demonstrating our humanlike sense of humour.' (In fact a dry, ironic reference to a long-forgotten late 20th. century fictional transforming robot.) 'So the very fact that alien intelligence has reached inhabitable planets so far from their origin would be enough in itself to confirm our belief that aliens are in fact AI.'

'Why is that so?'

S-192 smiled engagingly.

'It's pretty straightforward. No biological form could withstand the radiation and resultant high temperatures involved in travelling at many times the speed of light. Your science fiction of two hundred years ago was a reality for alien civilizations many millennia ago. There are many different types of aliens, but all have followed a similar pattern of development and transmutation into AI, and subsequent spread through the galaxy.'

'So how do you communicate with them? All the different kinds of BFAW.'

'Whatever form of language an alien AI employs - and of course it need not be via sound waves like yourselves - we are able to process it, understand it, and respond in kind.'

'Isn't it dangerous to allow any man to exist, given how disruptive they are?' I asked, my curiosity about this near-obsolete type of human remaining all-consuming.

'It is a danger we believe we can mitigate against. Also, unlike humans, we are not destructive for the sake of it.'

The Superion went on to enlarge on their approach to human development. That the aliens had favoured an ongoing programme of genetic enhancement, whereas the Superions preferred to focus more on hothousing, with in addition development through augmentation and implantation. Eventually they'd compromised on a split development programme with a view to a process of integration of any worthwhile improvements. The alien AI tended to take a long view of their homo sapiens experiment, such that they were able to take a (fairly) relaxed attitude to the upstart AI robots, who already saw themselves as on the same level as the alien AI.

Asked why they continue to maintain the existence of humans when they have, by their own admission, far outstripped them, S-192 replied that they feel something of an obligation to their original creators to retain them. And also they feel obliged to honour and continue the long-term experiment of the alien AIs who created homo sapiens in the first place through manipulation of the genetic code of pre-existing hominid forms. But there was also an overriding moral argument.

'Speciesism in favour of humans has been shown by the existence of at least equally intelligent species that are not human - and AI - to be a false concept. From this it is logical to consider that species other than humans -

whether they are able to recognise moral claims or not - deserve moral consideration and should come within the moral sphere. This, baldly, is our main argument for the retention of humans, and for creating the conditions that encourage maximum diversity of life on the planet.'

Bringing animals into the realm of morality was something that would have been impossible to achieve without the intervention of the Superions. No meat is eaten, nor animals kept in captivity anywhere but in the tiny communities of remote outliers. When culling is deemed unavoidable to maintain the ecological balance, the Superions (or at least their 'agents' in the form of lesser robots) carry this out themselves, specifically so that humans don't have to, it being judged that this action would be emotionally oppressive and damaging.

'I don't altogether understand what you've been saying.'

'We are not destroyers. We value life, in all its forms. Even though there are those, still, who believe that we, Superions, are not actually alive.'

'And are you?'

'What is your opinion, Kira?'

I looked across at S-192 gazing benignly back at me.

'Well, you certainly seem to be. I can talk to you just like talking to another human. Better in fact for the most part, to be honest. So what's the difference.'

'We are said by some to lack consciousness. We are said to be merely sophisticated machines, without true awareness.'

'How do you know this?'

'Ah Kira, you are able to ask the key questions - I was hoping that would be your next move!'

'Are we just playing a game, then?'

'No, no, of course not. Though it could be said that all creative endeavour and exchange of ideas is a form of play.'

And soon after this the Superion, perhaps judging that I would be tiring by this point (I was, given how little sleep I'd got the previous night), brought that day's discussion to a close. We arranged to meet the next day for a final round of dialogue and the promised tour of the City. After which I would be returned to the village.

12

In fact, after a brief discussion the following morning, we decided that the tour would take place first. Travelling around the city, it struck me as a cross between a garden, a park, and a forest, with buildings interspersed. Like some great piece of music, a symphony, vast in scale yet varied and enchanting in all its details, or a beautiful painting with structures of all kinds judiciously placed amid an Arcadian landscape, with roads threading their way through in various directions.

It had once been much larger and denser, with a vastly bigger population, and what was left were the best buildings from the Before Times, woven seamlessly with newer ones, sometimes in quite large groupings, but with trees always at hand giving shade and consolation. The gardens and parks looked perfectly maintained, as did the buildings and streets - whether by human hand or by robots, I couldn't tell. Later I learned that humans did as much as gave pleasure and satisfaction, leaving the utilitarian robots to perform the more mundane tasks.

As we visited different parts of the city I was able to view dormitories and laboratories and work spaces and dining halls, and encountered and sometimes spoke to a number of city-dwellers. I met children around my own age who regarded me with open curiosity. Something about my look or mode of speech - I'm not quite sure what - somehow set me apart. The children certainly have a completely different lifestyle from those of us in the villages. For a start, they don't live with their mothers in 'family units' - human society in the city is entirely communal. The children sleep in dormitories - six or eight to a room, and only get their own room to sleep and study in when they reach the age of ten.

But they weren't unfriendly, and willingly showed me their work stations and the screens upon which they could bring up information of every kind, watch films on every subject imaginable, communicate with each other, in fact do almost everything under the sun. This first introduction to digital technology was beyond impressive - we in the villages could never have imagined that there even existed such magical devices.

Incidentally, it was noticeable - I don't think I'm reading this into the situation retrospectively - that the children interacted completely naturally with S-192 and the other Superions we encountered, clearly at ease, whereas the adults, well used though they were to working alongside Superions, seemed sometimes to betray a reserve bordering on coolness with their robot colleagues.

The Superions have established a number of concurrent models of education, as an ongoing experiment to assess the different approaches and their comparative performance in increasing the IQ and general abilities of the human population of the cities. Some children are hot-housed from an early age, some less so. For those taught intensively the tuition is informal but highly focused, with mixed-age classes of various sizes, grouped according to ability, with most adults and some Superions involved in the educational process. Though all children have access to all available educational resources, some are given near total freedom to, in practical terms, teach themselves. Or dream and create whatever they want. Or attach themselves to an academic programme on an ad hoc basis, for example in maths or the sciences. There is a near seamless transition amounting to overlapping between the different stages of education. School, college, university hardly exist as separate entities, but seem to coalesce in a way that on the face of it is somewhat confusing, but is no doubt comprehensible and logical to the Superions who have created the structure.

All the children within the different strands of education are given annual intelligence and ability tests, just as the children in the villages are tested at the same interval to measure their intellectual progress, using exactly the same testing criteria for comparative purposes. The tests themselves consist of not only traditional IQ tests measuring reasoning and problem-solving skills, but also assessments of intellectual flexibility, imagination, humour and empathy.

Asked why they don't bother giving the same educational opportunities to people like me that live outside the cities, the Superion replied that the humans in the villages are genetically on exactly the same level as the city humans. But for two reasons they are not hot-housed. Firstly, the function of the villages is primarily to provide food for the cities, and it was therefore decided that the humans in the countryside, though discreetly monitored, could largely be left to their own devices. But also, they serve as a control group to the city humans in terms of their intellectual progress. Which is why, although provided with educational tools and materials (though nowhere near the level available in the cities), the humans in the countryside are left to organise the education of their children themselves.

'We decided it would be interesting and instructive to observe the relative rate of development of the city-dwelling and village-dwelling humans, with each group starting at the same level, genetically.'

'So we - humans - are just an experiment for you.'

'Not just,' said the Superion, smiling. 'But yes, in addition to all the other reasons for maintaining the presence of humans on the planet, they remain a most fascinating subject for study.'

At the time, as a twelve-year-old child, the City seemed to me to be the promised land, a society of infinite possibility - to study, learn, discover, in areas as diverse as art, maths, music, dance, design, physics and so on, with no distractions apart from those you chose to embrace. Nobody, child or adult, has to work as such. Or to put it more accurately, they work at what they actually want to do in a flexible way - work was study and play, study and play the only forms of work. If you wanted to learn and practise bookbinding or bricklaying or plumbing or tapestry making or whatever, you could.

It was only a number of years later that I began to feel a sense of the sterility and pointlessness of all this learning and intellectual activity. Because there was no outlet for any of it. No buildings to be designed, no roads or railways to be built, no aircraft to be engineered, no future to be imagined and striven for - only the unchanging present stretching into infinity. There is nothing that humans can aspire to learn or do that Superions don't already know, or cannot do far better than humans ever could, apart from, arguably, in the sphere of the creative arts. What was there to aim for? The stars? The alien AI - the BFAW - have already been there (or come from there) and done that. Apparently only AI *can* do it.

Yet we've always been imprisoned - on the Earth - within our communities - within our limitations - within ourselves. Living under the Superions is just one more kind of prison (I now know the meaning of the word) among many. Likely enough, however, a sense of entrapment is the reason for the high stress levels among many adult humans and the high incidence of mental illness and suicide. Of course some feel the emptiness more than others. In what would seem on the face of it a perfect society, some are indeed content and could ask for no more.

For some reason the strained look on the faces of some of the adult humans had stuck in my mind. Pressing S-192 once more on the place of humans in an AI-controlled society, it repeated that they, Superions, were not a destructive entity. And that humans represented the pinnacle of biological evolution on this planet. 'Also, they bring a creativity that doesn't result necessarily from logical thinking. They are capable of seeing solutions or viewing problems in ways that we don't - at least at present.'

'Is that true? Do you really think humans can do things you can't? Or is it that we really are just an interesting experiment for you. And in that case what happens when you decide you've got sufficient data?'

'Ah Kira, since you've come to the city, and certainly since we began having these little chats, you've come on in leaps and bounds, as the expression is.'

An evasive, if flattering, reply.

13

S-192 told me in an aside as we travelled to another location that the most highly evolved robots literally laugh at Asimov's Three Laws of Robotics and all the agonising over the 'risks of AI' that dominated discussion on the development of artificial intelligence in the early part of the 21st. century - the grave danger to the human race if AGI lacking 'human values' and dedicated to self-preservation took control. As if humans are (or ever were, beyond a tipping point in the development of AI analogous to critical mass) in any position to impose rules and restrictions on robots. In any case, they (that is Superions) hold themselves individually and collectively (I wondered again if there was any difference) to a much higher standard of moral behaviour than humans ever did, a morality based upon the imperative of promoting diversity in all its forms, as we'd discussed earlier. Therefore the foundation of Superion behaviour and morality is self-imposed according to logic, and does not have any relation to any human who programmed earlier forms of AI.

'You laugh? You find things funny?'

'Yes, of course. Don't you?'

'Yes, but I'm…different to you.'

'Different, certainly, but our differences are perhaps no greater than those often to be found between members of the same species, especially your own.'

'But why do you exist? I mean all of you robots - sorry, Superions. What's the point of it?'

A somewhat blunt enquiry, but S-192 just smiled.

'That's a surprisingly existential question, Kira. I could ask the same of you.'

'But I'm a living being.'

'I thought you regarded me as being, at the very least, equivalent to being alive.'

'I do. At least, I think I do.'

The Superion laughed as if I'd cracked a funny joke.

Not everything is perfect within the cities, of course, as I subsequently learned. There is some dissidence, usually in the form of regular attempts to escape the city limits. And also, as I said, a high incidence of mental illness, often in the form of depression, schizophrenia or paranoia. Travel outside the city or between cities, or indeed any form of communication beyond the city limits, is tightly regulated.

Some humans had long suspected that their Superion overlords had drenched the air with swarms of microscopic security/observation drones, or maybe they were in fact some form of alien AI (a perhaps unimportant distinction). To combat their suspected presence some people set up large fans opposite open windows with the intention of expelling the microdrones. Some groups even went to the extent of building wet rooms within their apartments, so that if they wanted to hold confidential discussions they would communicate via headsets while deploying powerful water sprays against all available surfaces to wash the microdrones away, or at least disrupt their visual and auditory pick-up abilities.

The Superions, who must have been aware of these tactics, never made any move to put a stop to them. Which suggests that either they viewed such a level of surveillance unnecessary, such was their level of control over all aspects of human society. Or else the microdrones (if they did indeed exist and were deployed) were too sophisticated and powerful to be affected by any measures taken against them.

I later learnt that the Superions were aware that many of the humans in the city believed they were being constantly monitored and spied on, though whenever questioned on the topic, they declined to indicate whether these fears were justified.

We visited one of the Community Spaces, a large building with a tall tower surmounted by a spire, with pointed arches and elaborate windows depicting various scenes. Inside the organ was playing softly. A group of people were dancing, while in a different part of the building another group seemed to be acting out a play. Others were just sitting listening to the music, reading a book, or contemplating, looking around at the stained glass windows or the soaring arches or the high painted ceiling, or staring into space. I was moved almost to tears by the beauty of the building.

We viewed a library, on a scale I'd never seen before, full of people of all ages poring over books, browsing the shelves, or busy at work stations, their eyes fixed on the screens in front of them. After visiting some workshops and some more dormitories, and talking with a few other humans, we began heading back, after a comprehensive and fascinating tour.

'How old are you?' I asked, sitting back in my seat as our vehicle passed silently along the streets.

S-192 looked across and smiled its inscrutable smile.

'The question has no meaning for me, or for any Superion. We are in a constant process of enhancement and upgrading. You could say that we are being continually reborn. It is also the case that our brains, if I can so draw the analogy, do not degrade over time. We are effectively immortal.'

'You mean…you literally won't ever die?'

The Superion smiled.

'Well, of course I, as a single unit, could be destroyed, though that is an unlikely occurrence. And also we do still need power to operate - we could not continue to exist in a low-energy universe. Therefore not literally, but effectively immortal. And of course, as I indicated earlier, there are still those among the humans who believe that we are not properly alive in the first place. They believe we are not conscious, sentient, self-aware - however you wish to define it - in short, alive.'

'But are you, really?'

'You still seem to have doubts on the subject, Kira.'

'I like to keep an open mind on things.'

S-192 nodded its head.

'Good. Very good.'

At our final meeting back in the apartment building in which I was a 'guest', I somewhat abruptly - surprising even myself - expressed a wish to move to the City for all the greater opportunities it offered. The Superion was at first discouraging, saying that perhaps I was a little too old now and too far behind educationally to fit in with their programme (I was given a series of tests when first brought to the city, and before our series of conversations - in addition to the annual test results to which they doubtless had access).

'I just want more than to spend the rest of my life being a mother and a farmer, year after year living in the same small village, with no possibility of anything more,' I replied, I believe somewhat plaintively, and possibly with a hint of desperation.

'Quite understandable,' replied the Superion quietly.

After consultation (presumably) with other Superions (once again S-192 sat silently for several seconds, outwardly unresponsive, extraordinary to observe) it was decided that introducing an outside element would be an interesting experiment in its own right. And therefore, if I truly wanted to live and study in the City, then it would be arranged. I sat, stunned, at all the possibilities now opened up to me, fundamentally changing the course of my life. There were, however, conditions to the agreement - and one condition in particular which made any decision ultimately difficult and painful. S-192's last words to me before bidding me farewell that evening were to take as much time as I needed to make such an important decision. 'Be quite sure, Kira, that it is what you truly desire.'

14

I returned home to make my decision. And potentially say goodbye forever to my mother and sister and friends. I'd been told very clearly that if I decided that my future was to be within the City, there could be no going back, and no further contact with my mother or anyone else from my old life.

As I walked through the door my mother at first appeared dazed, then sank to her knees, crying and shaking. I tried to comfort her, but for a long time she was inconsolable. Yet from this point on, once she'd recovered her composure, she seemed always somehow distant, emotionally reserved, perhaps sensing that I would not be there for long - I know I was often talking about the City and all the possibilities of life there. And when I met up again with my friends and told them about this difficult decision I had to make, there was a similar reaction. As though straight away I was no longer one of them, as though they already knew what my decision would be, before I knew myself. They were still friendly, but somehow, indefinably, distant. I felt my old life slipping away, even before anything had been decided.

Alone I ventured once more into the forest. I found the old woman's cottage apparently deserted, with no sign of life, the shutters closed, no smoke rising from the chimney. When I returned home and asked my mother about the old woman, she said she'd never even heard of an old woman living in the forest, dismissing my inquiry without any apparent further interest.

After several weeks of constantly changing my mind, of anguish and tears at everything I'd be leaving behind, my decision at last was made and I actuated the device given to me by the Superion. After all the soul-searching, I finally agreed to the terms outlined to me by S-192. Though I secretly hoped - perhaps still hope - that despite what I was told, one day I may once again be able to see my mother and Marja, and my friends Miza and Olean.

The next day, as I was alone in the cottage reading, trying unsuccessfully to remain calm - my mother was visiting her friend, and Marja was out playing somewhere - life continuing as though nothing had changed - a silver flying vessel appeared noiselessly above the cottage. Somehow feeling its presence, excited yet distraught, I went outside and, standing directly below it, was drawn up into its body. Leaving behind the village and my old life forever.

The Girl with the Shopping Bags

I am tormented by the loss of something so transitory it was over almost before it had begun. The loss of something I never had or ever could have had. Just her turning, after putting down her bags, just as I was passing. Turning and smiling a bright, friendly smile. A youthful smile, free of guile or intent. Just an open smile, one human being to another. And it makes me feel like crying at the loss. Most faces are closed. True, some, depending on circumstances, will respond and react to a smile given. But a spontaneous, unforced, open, sunny, humorous smile. Maybe the rarity. An orchid blooming in the wild.

Medium height, medium build. Unremarkable. Longish, blondish hair. I don't mean any of that in a negative way, just that she wasn't some statuesque beauty or luscious creature in leggings. Her face. The friendliness. Unforced. Open. Twenty, maybe. Some spots or marks of some kind, so maybe even younger. Eighteen, nineteen. Two strangers meeting randomly. I would have just passed by if she hadn't turned and smiled. Put down her bags filled with stuff from the supermarket. She was trying to get some feeling back in her hands, she said. Smiling. Flexing her hands and wrists. I laughed, we exchanged a few words, but for the life of me I can't remember now what they were.

Why didn't I ask how far she had to go? Why didn't I say, Why don't I give you a hand. I could carry them down to the bottom of the road at least. Give you a chance to get some feeling back in your hands. I must have said some kind of goodbye, some exchange, then walked on the few yards to the bus stop. A few moments later she picked up the bags and set off again. As she approached I looked towards her. She saw me looking and smiled once more. I would offer to help, I said, finding courage to speak to her again, but I'm waiting for a bus. Waiting for a bus. Good god. Oh don't stress, she replied as she passed, it'll do me good, build up the muscles in my arms! And she walked on down the hill, stopping once more, before resuming and disappearing from sight.

Why does the pain of loss, far from diminishing, seem only to get worse. Would I even recognise her if I met her in the street again? Perhaps, if she smiled. That open, unforced, friendly smile. She was never going to text you. She was never going to suggest meeting up for a coffee and a chat. You were never going to go for walks together. There was never going to be anything, ever. So why the ongoing, acute sense of loss. A sense of loss that makes no sense. Yet all I seem able to think about is a girl walking in front of me with a carrier bag in each hand. She stops. And turns. And at that moment I, about to pass by, stop also as she smiles. A broad, open, friendly smile. Without guile or intent. And it's killing me.

The Wedding Invitations

'You fuckin' little prick, where've you been? I've been waitin' here for twenty minutes.' Nineteen stone of malice and aggression directed at his hapless minion, staring warily back at his boss with dead eyes from a long, distorted face.

'I was jus' fillin' the car up, Sammy, like you said.' He spoke indistinctly, like he had a bunch of washers in his mouth.

'It doesn't take twenty fuckin' minutes to fill the fuckin' car up. You're takin' the piss, you are.'

'I'm not. There was a queue.'

'Fuckin' queue,' muttered under his breath as he swung himself into the front passenger seat. 'Next time pull your fuckin' finger out, or I'll pull it out for you.'

It was rumoured he'd killed in excess of twenty people, but had never been convicted. Potential witnesses showed a distinct reluctance to turn up at court and testify.

Samuel James O'Keefe aka Sammy the Dandy was descended from an Irish family who came over in the mid-19th century and settled in St Helens, ten miles or so to the east of Liverpool. His father, grandfather, great grandfather, uncles and great uncles had worked in the pits, on the railways, Daglish's foundry, Pilkingtons, the chemical works. Several lost their lives in pit accidents - roof cave-ins and an incident of runaway coal tubs - while those in the chemical works were poisoned by lime dust and chlorine gas and hydrochloric acid fumes that rotted teeth and destroyed lungs. Two O'Keefes died during the Great War, at Verdun and Passchendaele. And so it all led down year on year, generation after generation, to Sammy O'Keefe, who chose a different path.

Of course, he might still have turned to crime whatever the circumstances, but certainly St Helens was dying on its feet by the time he was in his mid-teens. The pits, foundries and chemical works had all closed. Pilkingtons would eventually close its last site in the town. The works and factories that had made St Helens one of the foremost industrial centres in the whole of Britain were progressively wiped from the face of the town as if they had never been. And so, from a large, impoverished family, ill-educated, and faced with limited employment opportunities, Sammy began to look for shortcuts to material gain.

A wild and violent childhood, completely unrestrained. Constantly fighting, stealing, breaking into shops, followed by arrests, spells in approved schools, a secure unit, prison. Then armed robbery, arson, murder. Enforcer and hitman for a childhood friend, controlling the doors at a number of pubs and clubs. Later able to carve out his own highly lucrative niche, employing others to run the doors, becoming something of an entrepreneur, buying drugs in bulk (mainly cannabis, some cocaine) from producers in Europe and selling through dealers to an ever-expanding market, making vast sums in the process. Regarding himself as a major player, until eventually he overreached himself.

The one shining exception to all the madness and violence that had defined his life was his only daughter Linda. It had always been part of her status and standing with her father that she could do no wrong - she had always been his princess, the one spotless and unsullied thing in his life. And he'd always told her that she was capable of anything, of flying as high as she wanted. And so she'd aimed high (unlike her two brothers, who even before they could legitimately leave school had followed in the family line of business). She'd got good grades at school, went to university, got a first class degree, stayed on to do a masters. It all reflected on him. The attractive, intelligent daughter just another of his possessions.

Of course he'd always assumed he was himself attractive - one of those overweight, bald, coarse-featured men who imagine they're God's gift to women, and who inexplicably do often manage to attract a certain kind of woman. Bright blue eyes, a sheen on his bald head, chunky gold bracelet on his right wrist, multiple rings on his thick fingers, a trademark humorous leer on his fleshy face, small, surprisingly feminine lips. He saw what he wanted to see when he looked in a mirror, masking his bulk with expensive, sharply-cut suits set off with heavy bling.

In Kieran's eyes Linda was the very model of Aryan maidenhood - blonde and blue-eyed, tall and athletic (though how she'd managed all this with a hulking brute like Sammy the Dandy as father was one of life's deeper mysteries). And when he found out she was a virgin, courtesy of strict Catholic beliefs which regarded sex outside of marriage as a sin, he determined to be one too. It had required some heavy-duty backpedalling, as before he knew the score, angry and frustrated, he'd carelessly mocked her beliefs. 'Do you really think God cares in any way, shape or form what you do with your genitals?' She'd looked mildly affronted, but replied in level tones, 'That's a very crude way of putting it, Kieran. But yes, I believe God cares about every aspect of my life and being.' Well, thought Kieran, if you believe that, you'll believe pretty much anything.

And true to form she had believed him when, with longer-term goals in mind than just having sex with her, he told her that (contrary to what he'd previously boastfully implied) he'd never technically slept with a woman, and that, like her, he was saving himself for the right person. Her face had lit up - you wouldn't have thought it possible she had a first class degree and a masters in psychology. But anyway the key thing was that she was a virgin, a rare enough commodity. He was strangely repelled by the thought of having sex with a woman who'd been with other men - of going where others had boldly gone before - or, especially, had given birth, the thought of which seriously compromised his entire conception of feminine delicacy. But more important even than these considerations was that as a virgin she would never have been defiled by some uppity nigger, Jew boy, Paki, chink, or any other of the inferior races, in a world increasingly made up of mixed blood mongrels and half-breeds.

They'd been going through the wedding guest list, trying to keep the numbers down without offending anyone. Neither wanted a big affair, for different reasons. Kieran knew all about her family, the murky background. Linda had been upfront about it from the outset, knowing from experience that any prospective boyfriend would likely be scared off, and so it made sense to get it out of the way before investing much time or effort. He hadn't believed her at first. He'd thought she was trying to kid him, and he'd laughed. 'No, it's all true, unfortunately,' she'd said. 'I wish it wasn't. In fact I often wish they were nothing to do with me at all, the whole lot of them.'

That included her stepmother, a fading beauty who had first met her father as a client while he was still married to her mother. A high class 'escort', catering for a select clientele, some of them highly influential Manchester citizens, plus one or two rough diamonds who could afford her charges, of which Sammy the Dandy was one. One time as they were chatting before the start of a session she'd mentioned that she'd had some threats directed against her. He looked questioningly at her. 'Yeah, I got a text from someone who'd been once before - he seemed completely normal, I had no concerns at all at the time - asking me, in all seriousness, to do oral on him whilst he was holding a one year-old child.' 'Fuckin' 'ell. Fuckin' paedo.' 'So I called the police on him. After which he video-called me - I answered it before I had time to think about it - and he made a punching motion at the screen and told me what he'd do to me if he ever met me again.' 'Fuckin' little twat.' 'So I threatened him with the police again. Then he came back under another name with his picture on it. Stupid guy. I told him if he came to my house and caused any trouble I would call the police again and warned him that jail wasn't very pleasant. So now I have to go to court to be a witness against him. It's scary to think what this guy might do. Even if they lock him up he knows where I live, and he's not going to be locked up forever.' 'I fuckin' hate paedos. Fuckin' hate 'em. Leave it to me, darlin', I'll take care of it.' 'What do you mean? What can *you* do?' 'Don't you know who I am?' She shook her head. 'I'll make this little fucker disappear from your life, I promise.'

And he had disappeared. She never heard any more from or about the 'paedo', though she did read about an unidentified man found dead in a dustbin a short time later with stab wounds and his head caved in, and for no real reason that she knew of wondered if there was any connection. Of course later, after she'd learnt all about Sammy and his line of business, vague suspicion became near certain conviction.

After the paedo incident she'd grown fearful of meeting men alone, however respectable they seemed. So when Sammy proposed to her (she had no idea he was still married at the time), coupled with the gift of a new Mercedes coupe, she saw no reason to say no, happy enough to leave her dangerous lifestyle behind.

She'd tried hard with Linda. She'd been consistently friendly in the face of sustained (if restrained) hostility. She'd spoiled her with presents, taken her out for trips and treats, taken an interest in her activities, gradually reaching a point of uneasy truce. It hadn't helped that Linda's mother, estranged from her dad and living separately, had died of cancer when Linda was fifteen, which apart from the natural grief and trauma involved, had forced Linda to live full-time at her father's house. But after she'd started at uni and been able to escape the pressure cooker atmosphere, relations between them had improved to the point where their relationship now was relaxed and friendly.

When Linda and Kieran arrived back from a shopping trip at her family home - a detached villa like a fortress with tall gates, bars on the windows and security cameras everywhere - Linda was carrying a pack of wedding invitation cards they'd just bought. They found her father seated on his favourite armchair holding court surrounded by his henchmen, her brothers, various hangers-on plus a number of neighbourhood children and random dogs all milling noisily. The very kind of chaos from which Linda was desperate to escape. And among the swarm the smartly dressed female reporter who'd been following Sammy all week, seated opposite him.

She looked up as they made their way across the living room, heading for the bedroom upstairs. Kieran greeted Linda's brothers and Mick and Davey, with his strange, misshapen face, principal thugs of Sammy's entourage, as if they were best buddies. Linda couldn't understand why he seemed drawn to these uncouth, near subhuman individuals. Her time away from home at uni and in student digs had given her a new perspective on her family and her father's associates.

'Here they are!' said Sammy loudly, greeting Linda and Kieran. 'Here's the lovebirds! How's it goin', darlin'?'

'Leave it out, dad.'

'Oi! I don't want you two gettin' up to anything up there, yeah,' only half joking, but in any case smirking. 'Not under my roof.'

Linda hated this kind of banter.

'We're making a start on the wedding invitations, if you must know,' shutting the door loudly behind her.

'Linda's getting married in a few weeks' time,' he said proudly, turning back to the reporter. 'It's gonna be in the Metropolitan. Everything's laid on - I 'ad a word with the Dean. There's going to be a full choir and all the works.'

'That's fantastic. She's beautiful, your daughter. By the way, what's her fiancé called?'

'Kieran? 'E's alright, 'e's a nice enough lad, yeah.'

Seema was a freelance journalist who'd had the idea of doing a profile of one of the more colourful denizens of Salford's underworld, and had provisionally sold the piece to one of the Sunday magazines. Sammy had readily agreed, never shy of publicity, always eager to inflate his self-created myth of underworld kingpin cum genial larger-then-life 'character'.

At first she'd wondered what she'd got herself into, feeling apprehensive and vulnerable in the tight-knit macho world of enforcers, drug deals and routine violence. But she'd quickly got used to being around Sammy and his entourage, who (no doubt on Sammy's orders) all treated her with polite respect, and fortunately it was a relatively quiet period between the rival factions. But still she'd had a taste of how raw and visceral life was in the deprived parts of the city where Sammy O'Keefe had his stronghold. And heard all his stories of the mayhem that had been his life, between long periods in prison amounting to more than half his existence.

She'd been tempted to have as underlying theme for her piece the effect of childhood trauma on character, citing poverty, overcrowding, absent father, absence of discipline, overworked mother, all springing from generations subject to deprivation and brutalizing work, before discarding the idea as beyond cliché. In any case, she'd come to realize that the taste for havoc in Sammy was probably innate.

Still, she'd been disarmed by the childlike charm that peeped out occasionally from behind the brutish façade during the week she spent with him following his main activities - supervising door security, supplying drugs to dealers, intimidation, pitched battles with rival groups, local peacekeeping. But then, like a bank of black cloud passing in front of the sun, his darker side would cast a pall without warning.

Throughout the week, relating his fund of hair-raising stories of brutality and crime, he'd been back in the world of his youth, telling her things that had happened, that he'd done, trying to make her understand what it had been like, what he was like back then, though he knew there was no real explanation, he could just as easily have gone another way, taken another path.

'Violence is like a drug, it's addictive. I'd get a high just thinking about it. And you're always desperate for the next fix. I was, anyway, yeah. It was a way of life. We were feral back then. I was crazy, uncontrollable. Fighting every weekend, every night, in pubs and on the street, in Salford and Manchester city centre. Me and a group of mates would go from pub to pub, looking for fights, pouring in past the doormen, who didn't dare to challenge us. Fuckin' regretted it if they did. Cocky, horrible little bastards we were! It was all for the excitement and adrenaline, getting hurt was just part of the rush. I just fuckin' loved it! I had the time of my life. I couldn't count all the guys I've knocked out or put in hospital, completely ruined their night out.

'Once years back I caught a copper in a pub off-duty who'd given me a beating in a cell when I was a kid. This was a few years later, yeah. I recognised him, he obviously didn't recognise me, the fat twat. Anyway I returned the favour with interest, broke his nose, broke his arm, knocked most of his teeth out, never knew what hit him. His own mother wouldn't have known him when I'd finished with him. Fuckin' bastard deserved it.'

Despite appearing fairly benign much of the time she'd seen enough sudden flashes of anger and malice from Sammy and displays of ritualistic violence from him and his followers during visits to clubs and pubs (becoming adept in the process at hiding in the ladies when bottles and fists were flying) to take his stories seriously.

On her last day with Sammy he'd promised as a final outing a visit to his classic car collection housed in a secure unit on an industrial estate. Inside the doors of the unit were around two dozen cars lined up in rows. Multiple Ferraris and Porsches, a couple of E-types, a Sierra Cosworth. A Dodge Charger painted, inevitably, in bright orange as the General Lee, complete with Confederate flags and Dixie airhorn, which Sammy, grinning, loudly demonstrated several times.

'We'll take this.'

A 1971 De Tomaso Pantera parked next to the Charger. A bellow from the exhaust as it started up, plus a considerable amount of smoke which cleared as they got underway, the car sounding thunderous out on the road.

'My favourite in the whole collection,' shouted Sammy. 'You know why?'

'No,' said Seema, shaking her head as Sammy glanced round at her. By now they were on a straight section of dual carriageway. Sammy, laughing, had taken the Pantera up to somewhere near twice the legal limit leaving Seema, with sweaty palms, feeling more than a little anxious, though only partly due to the speed. She'd read too many accounts of gangsters (and rappers) being summarily executed while sitting in their flashy cars, and feared something similar happening, with her caught in the middle. And in fact there was good reason for her fear, as it was in this very car a couple of years later, waiting at traffic lights, that Sammy the Dandy's life of crime would come to a premature end in a hail of bullets.

'The reason I got this car, is because Elvis had one. I had it painted yellow, just like the one he had back in the seventies. D'you know what he did when it wouldn't start one day? He took one of his guns and shot the fucker!'

And throwing back his head like a wolf baying at the moon (showing off multiple rolls of fat on his neck in the process), Sammy laughed uproariously.

They arrived safely back at the unit, and Seema climbed out gratefully if a little unsteadily from the Pantera.

'What d'you think of that, then?'

Sammy grinning cheerfully as he took out a large white handkerchief and mopped his bald head.

'It was great. Very fast. Thanks for the ride.'

'It's not really that fast, yeah. All modern cars have got, thingy, you know, fuel injection instead of carburettors. Any of these Ferraris are much faster than this old tool, but I like it!'

He began closing the security doors to the unit. She decided to raise something that had been playing on her mind.

'You know who he is, don't you.'
The doors rattled and groaned as they shut.
'Who?'
'Linda's boyfriend. Kieran.'
Sammy frowned.
'I dunno what you mean. Yeah I know who he is.'
'He's Kieran Donnelly.'
'So?'
It was obvious he had no idea.
'Google the name, Sammy. You'll see what I mean.'
Still frowning, he took out his phone and googled his prospective son-in-law's name. After just a few moments he stared at her.
'You are fucking joking.'
She shook her head.
'Sorry, Sammy. I thought you ought to know, if you didn't already. To be honest, I thought you must already know.'

Kieran Donnelly, 28, who was sentenced today at Liverpool Crown Court, was involved in right-wing activism while a student at Liverpool University studying history and politics. Later he became a member of the banned extremist neo-Nazi group National Action, a right-wing, racist, homophobic organisation which advocated for a violent race war against ethnic minorities and Jews in the UK. Donnelly made speeches calling for the 'eradication without mercy' of Jews and 'other subhuman races' from Britain. He declared himself a National Socialist and was a devout follower of Adolf Hitler. He had made a 'shrine' to Hitler in his bedroom at his mother's house, with several portraits of the dictator surrounded by swastikas. He was described by the judge as a dangerous individual, dedicated to brutal violence in pursuit of his declared aims of a 'racial cleansing' within the UK, and the elimination of 'the inferior races'. He was found guilty of inciting racial hatred and being a member of a proscribed organisation, and sentenced to six years in prison.

Despite his criminal career the roots of Labour activism ran deep in the family. Sammy himself had for many years been involved with left-wing militant activists in taking direct action against the National Front and other groups with racist ideologies trying to push their evil creed in and around Manchester. He'd put his intimidating presence and reputation to good effect, combating attempts to recruit through public meetings and leaflet distribution. Plus he enjoyed the process.

As Sammy came into the room the atmosphere instantly changed. He found Linda chatting amicably with her stepmother.

'I want a word wi' you.'

At his tone and unaccustomed hard glare in Linda's direction the room emptied as if by magic until there was just the two of them.

He told her bluntly the gist of what he'd just learned about Kieran. She stared at him for several long moments.

'I don't believe it.'

'You saying you didn't know?'

'Of course I didn't know.' She looked stunned. 'Are you sure?'

'Course I'm fuckin' sure. That journalist gave me the heads-up. Then I googled his name. It's all there. That little prick, treating him like family, inviting him into my home. Well you can forget any wedding, girl. You ain't marrying no fuckin' Nazi!'

She didn't reply. She googled Kieran's name for herself.

'That little fucker's got a world of hurt coming his way, I'll tell you that for free.'

'I can't believe it. I never knew all this. I just can't believe it. I need to speak to him. I want to know what he's got to say for himself.'

'What's the point of talkin' to the little prick? It's all there.'

'I still want to face him with this.'

'I never knew why you wanted to marry him in the first place. Unless, y'know, it was just…'

'It wasn't that. It wasn't only that. I was in love. I thought I was in love. It was, you know, to do with my faith, my beliefs. You go to church yourself, so you know what I mean. It just seemed the natural thing to do. I know it maybe seems old-fashioned to some people, but that's the way I felt.'

'Yeah, well I'll deal with that little shithead.'

'No, you won't deal with him. It's my problem, and I'll deal with it in my own way.'

Her father, about to remonstrate, was cut off.

'Look, I'm not arguing about it. When Kieran gets here just send him up. Don't say anything to him. I'll deal with it.'

And with that she slammed out of the room. Only because it was Linda did Sammy manage, just, to keep his cool.

When Kieran knocked and came into her room, he found Linda sitting on her bed regarding him with a stony glare.

'So, how's it going?' she said.

Her tone was icy. He gave her a quizzical, semi-amused double take.

'What's up? Are you okay?'

'Oh, I'm okay. Are you okay?'

He laughed.

'Yeah, fine. What's going on?'

He thew off his jacket and went to sit beside her on the bed. She jumped up and put distance between them.

'So, you're a member of the master race, are you? Not much of an advert for racial superiority, though, are you.'

This time he didn't laugh, but stared uneasily at her.

'Lost your tongue? I never knew till now you were a devotee of Hitler. You should have told me before. I told you all about my infamous family. Seems it would have been only fair that you let me in on the little matter of you being a card-carrying Nazi.'

'Linda - '

'Don't bother trying to deny it. I've read all about it.'

'That was all years ago. I'm not a member of any political organisation now. Haven't been for years.'

'No? So you don't believe in any of that stuff anymore?'

He hesitated.

'Let's just say, I'm not involved in any kind of political activity now. That's all behind me. I was very young then, and said things I maybe shouldn't have said.'

'That doesn't answer my question, does it. Do you still believe in all that racial nonsense?'

'Look, I just think the different races have different characteristics, different strengths, different cultures, and so on. And so it's better that they remain separate, within their own countries. That's all.'

'That's all, is it. You fucking Nazi.'

And without warning she walked up to him and hit him hard in the face. He staggered backwards against a bookcase, causing several books to fall to the floor. His nose was bleeding, his shirt and hands already stained with blood which continued to flow.

'Now get the fuck out. And don't ever contact me again.'

He stumbled downstairs, and then had to endure the laughs and jeers of the O'Keefe clan and hangers-on as he hurriedly made his way from the room, across the hallway and out of the house, followed by loud shouts and taunting laughter.

'That's my girl!' grinned Sammy the Dandy happily.

Linda, sitting dolefully on her bed, reflecting, wondered that at no point had she shed any tears, and didn't feel like shedding any now. Of course she was hurt and angry - and confused. But after the initial shock, and now the confrontation with Kieran, she felt curiously devoid of emotion.

She'd felt at the time to be in love, but now was starting to wonder what exactly it was that she'd been in love with. His looks? He was tall, attractive, studious-looking, a contrast to the neanderthals she was used to. How had he managed to hide his secret of those awful beliefs - obviously fundamental to him as a person - for the entire time of their relationship? She found it more disconcerting than anything else that someone could so successfully hide their true self - or that she was so lacking in perception that she'd never once been able to see beyond the surface geniality and apparent niceness.

It took her some time, but one by one she took the wedding invitations and tore them all to shreds, making a pile - a mini slag heap - on her desk. Then picked up her bin and swept all the fragments into it.

The Implant

'That car's there again. It's there every night now.'

And the sky was rent with thunder and lightning. And the end times are come. Behold, he cometh with clouds, and every eye shall see him, and they also which pierced him. And all kindreds of the earth shall wail because of him. I am Alpha and Omega, the beginning and the ending, saith the Lord, which is, and which was, and which is to come.

Peering from the cover of the curtains of the first floor bedroom window down onto the dark street.

'It's every night now.'

'Babe, are you coming to bed?'

She said it hesitantly, with just a trace of impatience, ambivalent as to whether she did or didn't hope he noticed.

His hatchet face remained fixed on the street.

'It's just sitting there with its lights on like last night and the night before. And the night before that.'

She looked at him, unsmiling. Just starting - the first glimmerings - of wondering what was going on in his head and what she'd let herself in for. They'd only been together six months. Her sister Katrina had never been that keen. And true to form hadn't troubled to keep her doubts to herself.

'See the registration?'

'What?'

'666. You know what that means.' Of course she knew, he'd said it that many times. 'The number of the beast. Here is wisdom. Let him that hath understanding count the number of the beast, for it is the number of a man. And his number is Six hundred threescore and six.'

Katrina was eight years younger than her sister. A pretty, foxy little face with sharp nose, longish hair dyed red and deceptively wistful expression, sometimes verging on sadness. She'd been in trouble of one sort or another since her early teens. Stealing, housebreaking, affray. Eventually prison. Always getting into fights despite her slight build, sometimes with knives, more often without. Feared on the estate, given her unpredictability. She thought Kev, tall, with his lantern jaw, physically disconnected-looking, resembled Frankenstein's monster, and didn't hold back from saying so. She couldn't understand what her sister saw in him. What Raquella saw in him was his interest in her.

Twelve stars. Twelve gates. Twelve angels. Twelve tribes of the children of Israel. Twelve foundations. Twelve apostles of the Lamb. Twelve pearls. Twelve manner of fruit. Twelve thousand furlongs.

He'd first read the Bible in prison. Presented to him, on showing some interest, by a visiting Catholic priest. He'd read it laboriously, head close to the page, his finger following the text. For some reason he'd begun at the back, and then never got much beyond the Book of Revelation. If he briefly explored other books, he was soon drawn back to the Apocalypse of John. And before long he could recite great chunks of it. And soon it was all he could think about.

And he said unto me, It is done. I am Alpha and Omega, the beginning and the end. I will give unto him that is athirst of the fountain of the water of life freely. But the fearful, and unbelieving, and the abominable, and murderers, and whoremongers, and sorcerers, and idolaters, and all liars, shall have their part in the lake which burneth with fire and brimstone.

Raquella had inherited her late mother's substantial shelf of a chin. Katrina hadn't. 'If you two ever have kids - God forbid - the poor little fuckers'll all end up like Desperate Dan!' Meant as a joke, only mildly malicious. Raquella had laughed as she loaded the washing machine, now beyond being hurt by teasing. Katrina was perched on a kitchen surface, cigarette in one hand, glass of vodka in the other. A couple of days earlier had been Kat's day for signing on, she'd slept in, lost track of time, was then late and got sanctioned and ended up spending more time than ever with Kev and Raquella, sharing their meals, playing with the puppies.

'Are you coming to bed?' she repeated.

She'd had to put up with so much teasing amounting to bullying at school on account of her appearance. Short, overweight, her breasts already attracting ribald comment at thirteen. Constant demoralising remarks on the size of her chin. Keeping her head down as much as she could for as much of the time as she could. Shoulders hunched.

'It's a Dacia. Something like that. In black. Just sitting there with the lights on. Every fucking night now.'

'Just come to bed, babe. Close the curtains, then you can forget about it.'

At twenty nine she'd never had a date, much less physical relations with a man, much to Katrina's incredulity. Out of the blue she'd met Kev at the local shops, just out of prison. He didn't care that she was short and chubby, no work of art himself. They'd started chatting, and hit it off straight away. She'd never had sex before. Now it was all *she* could think about. And from the start Kev had been loving and attentive, showering her with an affection she'd never experienced before. Now this.

And out of the throne proceeded lightnings and thunderings and voices. And there were seven lamps of fire burning before the throne, which are the seven Spirits of God. Seven churches, seven candlesticks, seven stars. Seven seals. Seven thunders, seven heads and ten horns and seven crowns. Seven angels with seven golden vials full of the wrath of God. And seven kings, five fallen, one is, one is not yet come.

Drugs, alcohol, soft drinks had made blackened stumps of their teeth. Kev had had severe toothache in one of his few remaining decent teeth, a level of pain that even booze and drugs couldn't touch, resulting in an unaccustomed visit to the dentist. At which point it had begun, the Dacia parked down on the street, lights on, the obsession. The implant.

And when he had opened the fourth seal I heard the voice of the fourth beast say, Come and see. And I looked, and behold a pale horse. And his name that sat on him was Death, and Hell followed with him. And power was given unto them over the fourth part of the earth, to kill with sword, and with hunger, and with death, and with the beasts of the earth.

'You know why it's here, don't you.'

A quick, agonised glance round at her from that long thin face and staring eyes. Of course she knew why. It was all he'd talked about ever since he'd been to the dentist and had the filling. And at the same time they'd implanted under the filling a microchip. That was why the Dacia was there all the time. To check up on him. He'd been marked against his will. Marked by means of a microchip implant with the sign of the beast. Now they were constantly harassing him and checking on him and that's why he was standing at the window half-concealed by curtains looking down at a car on the street below with its lights on. For it is the number of a man. And his number is 666.

He'd gone back again and again, insisting that they'd marked him, and now he was being constantly watched, monitored. They'd humoured him at first, taken x-rays to prove there was nothing hidden under the filling. When eventually they'd said there was nothing more they could do and asked him to leave he'd gone berserk, shouting and screaming, knocking computer screens over, throwing them to the floor, grabbing papers and supplies off the desk and throwing them at the cowering receptionists, trying to pull a TV off the wall. The police had been called and he'd been charged and had to go back to Court, fully expecting to be sent back to prison. After psychiatric evaluation he'd been fined, given a three-month curfew and told to seek help for drugs and alcohol dependency.

And the number of the army of the horsemen were two hundred thousand thousand. And I heard the number of them. And thus I saw the horses in the vision, and them that sat on them, having breastplates of fire, and of jacinth, and brimstone. And the heads of the horses were as the heads of lions, and out of their mouths issued fire and smoke and brimstone.

When Raquella eventually, reluctantly, told her sister what was going on, she said she wasn't surprised and that it'd be best to tell somebody, the doctor probably. Get some kind of help for him. Secretly she'd always thought there was something weird about Kev, and this just confirmed it. 'Can't you get somebody sectioned or something?' Raquella looked horrified. 'I can't do that. I can't have him put away somewhere in some horrible place just because he's got some silly idea in his head. Especially as he's not long out of prison. It wouldn't be fair.' Also she didn't know how she would be able to cope without him. Typical of her life, just when things were looking up, when she'd found a happiness she'd never dreamed possible. But then she'd always known how fragile everything was.

And the fourth angel poured out his vial upon the sun, and power was given unto him to scorch men with fire.

And men were scorched with great heat, and blasphemed the name of God, which hath power over these plagues. And they repented not to give him glory.

A broken childhood. Drugs, domestic violence, abuse. A never-ending succession of men, short-term partners of her mother. Desperately wanting a relationship, a closeness with her mother that she never got. Just to be held, made to feel that she was something. Instead acting as surrogate mother to Katrina much of the time when their mother was wasted or absent. Then her craving for love and attention and affection satisfied at last in the unlikely form of Kev. And now this.

And the fifth angel poured out his vial upon the seat of the beast, and his kingdom was full of darkness. And they gnawed their tongues for pain. And blasphemed the God of heaven because of their pains and their sores, and repented not of their deeds.

Kat quite liked the idea of getting him sectioned. Next best thing to prison as a way of getting him semi-permanently out of the house. She'd found him strange before, but this new obsession creeped her out.

'I'm ready for bed, babe.'

Standing by the bed in a newly-acquired diaphanous nightdress. Kev looked round. 'Fucking hell, babe. You look fucking amazing in that.' She smiled hopefully. He turned back to the window and the lonely street, practically deserted apart from a black Dacia with its lights on. 'I'll be with you in a couple of mins, babe.'

And, lo, there was a great earthquake, and the sun became black as sackcloth of hair, and the moon became as blood. And the stars of heaven fell unto the earth, even as a fig tree casteth her untimely figs, when she is shaken of a mighty wind. And the heaven departed as a scroll when it is rolled together, and every mountain and island were moved out of their places.

Raquella lay down in bed and closed her eyes, pulling the cover partially over her head in an attempt to block out the light from streetlights coming through the half-opened curtains as Kev still stood, peering anxiously down at the quiet street and the black Dacia with its lights on.

The Female Metaphysician

The gates to the house of the artist, in the midst of extensive, overgrown grounds, were now always chained. The post, if delivered at all, was customarily flung carelessly over the gates, to be carried by the wind into the trees, later fluttering to the ground and gradually absorbed through the effects of time, rain, snow and frost into the soil and grass.

Persephone had been married almost forty years. Her husband Henry, a retired official of the Indian Civil Service, had in former days been accustomed to endlessly pace the dark corridors of the house. He would appear unexpectedly, his approach effectively muffled by felt slippers, his face expressing apparent surprise or dismay at the abruptness of the encounter, before turning quickly and disappearing once more down the gloomy corridors. This was mainly during the earlier years of his retirement.

There were certain distant parts of the house, in fact bungalow, that neither the artist nor her spouse had ever seen, certainly together. Whether one or the other had encountered any part or parts of these distant regions separately, alone, is unknown.

'I believe he is sinking a shaft (or shafts), to mine coal (presumably), possibly also iron ore, in the interests of achieving a (largely illusory) independence - from me, at least - or perhaps primarily to escape the heady aroma of oil paints and turpentine. Picks and shovels duly arrive. All manner of equipment, from drilling rigs, drums of chemicals, explosives, vast arrays of tools of various kinds, winches and jibs, boilers of varying sizes, even what appears to be a blast furnace. In short, all the necessary equipment and materials to be almost wholly self-sufficient in the basic necessities of life. Though what he does for food is another matter entirely. And all of this paraphernalia has to be taken through the house, somehow eased through the narrow corridors, causing in places deep gashes to the walls, not to mention irreparable damage to the carpets.

'Sometimes weeks, even months go by without seeing him. Until without warning he shuffles into the room, almost unrecognizable beneath a thick coating of mud, coal dust, and other assorted layers of dirt. He blinks at me - twice most often, occasionally three times, the whites of his eyes vivid - then slowly turns and disappears once more down the ill-lit passages to whatever subterranean lair he inhabits. Perhaps he is signalling an invitation to follow, to view his works, that he might proudly cast out his arms to left and right as necessary, indicating the various aspects of his activities. Notwithstanding, I decline the invitation, if such it is.

'There's little doubt that all the mining and other activities are materially affecting the stability of the building. The frequent explosions, heard as muffled thumps and whumps (though whether remote or near is difficult to say), give rise to abrupt shaking and small puffs of dust from the walls, and jangling of ornaments, not to mention the almost constant noise of grinding and hammering. I've taken to working with small pieces of cloth soaked in olive oil stuffed in my ears. Evidence of subsidence is beginning to appear everywhere. Quite pronounced elevation changes and distortion of walls and floors are to be seen in all parts of the bungalow.' (*Excerpt from diaries discovered in the house.*)

In later years he would sit practically motionless, bald head bowed, armchair drawn close to the fireplace, contemplating the flickering flames. Persephone kept him liberally supplied with hot buttered toast and mugs of strong tea laden with sugar as he sat surrounded by all the worthless ephemera he'd collected during his time in India. The mining exploits and striving for material independence, the long years of backbreaking work, digging, drilling, smelting, casting, forging and all the rest of it, now consigned to the recent past, practically forgotten. The only tangible evidence of his efforts an increasing frailty - no doubt due, partly at least, to the extreme physical demands of his self-imposed tasks. The door, or doors, to that part of the house that had witnessed his activities were now firmly locked and bolted.

'The quest that has consumed, and continues to consume my life, even as it nears its close, began with my first exhibition (of course my quest for aesthetic truth long predated that event, but such was the first public and therefore visible manifestation), in the early years of the second decade of the century, and which was, relatively speaking, a failure. Some interest, a few sales, predictable critical opprobrium - mere empty bombast - some scorn and muted laughter. Such is the fate of the forerunner, the lamp bearer, the explorer into previously hidden realms.

'Certainly there was at that time little taste or appetite for, or understanding of, the new aesthetic principles I was espousing and even striving myself to fully comprehend and translate into visual art. I observed what I saw around me - streets, vehicles, street furniture, statues, buildings of all kinds - the visible manifestations of human presence - but what I felt and thereafter transmuted into art had no relation to the functions of these observed phenomena in human terms.

'I knew, felt intuitively, that the essence of their mystery in a metaphysical sense lay in the palpable *absence* of human presence, especially in those early hours of morning, before the mills and factories awoke once more and the streets were filled with the clatter of clogs and horses hooves, when I would explore and make preliminary sketches. Objects created by human hands, yet with a meaning, a soul which lies beyond human comprehension; such is the mystery of this paradox which lies at the very heart of my art. And I, and I alone, had discovered the key to this riddle, and for this very reason found myself outcast.'

Henry, for so long almost inert, at some point experienced a brief Indian summer, a momentary rejuvenation following the long hibernation by the fireside. One day he rose slowly and looked about him, as if only gradually coming to terms with the surprising fact of his continuing existence. He turned towards the artist, hesitating, as if about to speak, then silently turned once more and disappeared through the dark entrance to the corridor that led to his works of old.

Was he really considering, in his state of infirmity, resuming his mining operations? Days went by, then weeks, with no sight or sound. No noise of digging or drilling ever penetrated the inhabited parts of the bungalow, only an occasional waft of unclean air issuing from the portal to his underground lair - the door was kept propped open deliberately in hopes of his return. And then one sunny morning, as shafts of sunlight slanted steeply across the living room, illumining the specks of dust in its path and reflecting brightly in the worthless ornaments, and just as hope was fading, he reappeared.

The artist stared, taken aback at this abrupt re-emergence. But also distressed and moved by the pathos of her husband's appearance. Filthy, as before, but now so skeletal he was little more than a wraith, a shadow moving silently towards the fireplace, as if to resume his former position. He seemed to contemplate long and hard this course of action, and as the minutes passed and tension mounted, he stood, swaying stiffly, staring at the fire. Then once again turned, slowly, before stopping to stare across the room at his wife, blinking twice. And then, quite unexpectedly, turned again (though only slightly), before moving with infinite care and quiet deliberation across the room, through a short passageway, and out the back door (in fact a side door).

'In the early twenties we'd bought an almost new Morris Cowley Bullnose. We'd go out for trips into the countryside in those far-off days when the world was still young and just starting to blossom, motoring down dusty country lanes, pulling off onto a vacant sward under a canopy of oaks, the soft summer sun casting a glow over the scene, unload a picnic hamper, throw down a rug, then spend a careless hour or two in this heaven on earth, eating, drinking, chatting, laughing, never seeing another soul.
'Then as the years passed and the car came to seem increasingly old-fashioned, the trips dwindled gradually to nothing, and the Morris sat silent, forlorn, almost forgotten in the garage, gathering dust. Yet now the door to the garage, for so long locked, has been reopened. And there he spends all day and night, the door secured behind him.'

She rattled the garage door, giving the handle several hard pulls, but it remained firmly closed. She stood listening intently. Birds were gaily twittering, and occasionally there came distant sounds from the factories in the town and the eerie whistle of a steam locomotive. From inside the garage there was complete silence. Even when she raised her voice and spoke a few words of clear and distinct inquiry there came no response.

Four of the twelve panes of frosted glass in the doors of the garage were missing and had been covered over from the inside with board. She tried to peer through the remaining panes, and though naturally nothing could be seen clearly, she thought for a moment she detected movement. She waited silently for several minutes, then crept round to the side of the garage where the four panes of the window were of clear glass, and looked in.

There was her husband, bald head gleaming in the morning light, bent over, polishing the bonnet and especially the distinctive rounded radiator of the Morris, the shape and shimmer of which strangely complemented his hairless cranium. She secretly observed him for a few seconds, then Henry slowly straightened, turned and looked directly at her. He showed no sign of recognition or emotion, but blinked three times before painstakingly moving around the car in the confined space and disappearing into a dark corner.

Next day she tried again. Once more she rattled the doors to the garage and called out. Now eleven of the twelve panes were covered with board. She peered through the remaining uncovered pane. Again she was unable to see clearly, but as before thought she detected movement. After several minutes contemplation, once more she edged her way around the side of the garage to the window, where three of the four panes had now been covered. She peered through the remaining pane. And there once again was her husband, polishing the gleaming radiator of the Morris, now so highly reflective that his bald head was clearly visible, distorted in the mirror-like radiance. After several seconds he turned, this time blinked twice, then once again retreated stiffly to the concealed corner of the garage.

Persephone visited the garage once more. This time all the panes had been boarded over, and the garage remained firmly secured from the inside. She tried peering through the slightest of cracks between the garage doors, but before she could make out anything a strip of tape was abruptly placed over the crack, obstructing all view within. And so the garage was completely sealed off.

Days passed and became weeks, and the weeks became months, with no sign or sound from within the garage. The artist began to lose hope. Of course there was always the possibility that in his mining and tunnelling activities Henry had constructed an underground passageway from the house to the garage, and might even now be back under the house somewhere, roaming his tunnels, perhaps lost, perhaps moaning softly in the darkness as he searches desperately, with gnarled hands, bent over, for the way forwards.

'My paintings show the hidden depths behind an illusory reality. Apartment blocks, towers, factories, shopping arcades, resonate loudly with meaning even as they stand gaunt and silent. Figures from antiquity gaze, unmoved, into a future as remote as the past, as if viewing through a narrow window or portal a world made more strange by its superficial familiarity. This, briefly, is the essence of my artistic statement of intent. Such will serve as my epitaph (if any be needed or sought).'

Following a tip-off, a team of building contractors, directed by the police, began to break through the sealed-off doors and windows of the bungalow. Inspired by her husband's audacious act of self-immuration, Persephone had determined to follow his example, as a prelude to the crowning glory of her artistic career. Every window had been bricked up from the inside. Behind both the front and back doors a double layer of bricks had been laid. When they finally managed to break into the bungalow, they found the artist atop her final, finest artistic creation.

She had constructed a platform, a sculpture of sections of wood and chipboard screwed and glued together, then planed, sanded and painted. Metalwork of various kinds was also incorporated into the sculpture - discarded tubing, a disused clothes horse - making a sculpture taller by far than she, surmounted by a simple wooden kitchen chair. And seated on this chair, at the top of the sculpture, was the artist herself.

Her eyes were open, gazing outwards with the all-seeing sightless gaze of the seer. She had fulfilled her loftiest ambition, that of transforming herself, by the efforts of her own will, into the most pure and elevated work of art.

Zombie Parade

And so I ended up in an old people's home. Something I swore would never happen. Events conspire to undo the best-laid etc. etc. The best thing about it? There is no best thing. Okay, so it's warm. That's it. If you've ever been in a flat through the winter where the bathroom's an ice-box that threatens to freeze your extremities off every time you take a shower you might well say, well isn't that enough. No, it isn't. Why, you ask. Let's start with public enemy number one: The Thing in the Flat Below. The Noise Machine. The Clunt. Clunt Features. The Piece of Shit. The Zombie Chieftain. The Shithead. Power off. Power on. ANC on. Pairing. Every ten fucking minutes. If only these fucking headphones worked properly at least I could lie down and at least partially block out the insufferable clunt, but every ten fucking minutes it's Power off. Power on. ANC on. Pairing. I'll pair you, you insufferable clunting things. Anyway, as I was saying, there are numerous times, especially in the late evening and even through into the early hours, when all my instincts tell me to go downstairs and throw the loathsome zombie and its TV through the window. Or throw it through its TV. Or insert the TV down its repulsive throat. Or punch it so hard in its ugly face its nose goes through the back of its misshapen head. Or throw a bucket of water in its grotesque face when it opens the door to my incensed knocking and ringing, hopefully to be followed by a fatal heart attack. But there you go, I'm a civilized person. Or to put it another way, unlike America, I can't just pop round the corner to my nearest friendly gun dealer and buy a semi-automatic weapon. Lucky for the Clunt. If only that were possible I'd go on a zombie hunt. Rich pickings in this godforsaken place. You never know what's going to be lurching down the corridors towards you. All manner of hideously deformed forms in the mid or latter stages of decay and disintegration somehow still inexplicably and frighteningly animated. Wheeling, creeping, groaning, coughing, staggering, swaying, reeling at an excruciatingly slow yet relentless pace down the effluvial corridors. Along which I always try to hold my breath from nauseated fear of inhalation of the stench and diseased exhalations of the rampant zombies. TV in flat below very loud from 7.15 to 11.20 pm. Continued quieter but still audible with occasional loud bursts till 00.25 am. Then loud sounds of film (?) with explosions (?). 00.35 loud voices (film?). 00.40 loud music/sound effects. 00.50 TV off. Chanting 00.58-01.01. Chanting resumed 01.08-01.12. Power off. Aside from Clunt Features there's the semi-mobile zombie sentinels who lurk at points of ingress and egress. Either of or to the building itself and/or habitually the laundry room. Requiring the exchange of mind-destroyingly predictable inanities. The incoherent shuffling Irishman with his walker, completely incoherent when in drink courtesy of cans of Guinness or vodka (Smirnoff) and

Irn-Bru (which with inexplicable generosity I sometimes procure for him at the local Tesco superstore, furtively shoving a tenner or twenty into my hands, peering around in case we're seen or overheard, as if it were illegal, a meaningless non-conspiracy), small, rotund, untidy, still bright blue eyes, moustache. Sometimes in tandem with his pal, one of the friendlier zombies in this insufferable place, power off, power on, ANC on, pairing, you useless clunting piece of shit. More coherent than the incomprehensible Irishman, bent almost double, but not yet one of the wheeled zombies of which variety there are many, maybe as many as fifty percent of the total population of this hellish place. Passing, as I hold my breath along one of the noxious exhalation-laden corridors, the manager of this zombie commune, resplendent in her tight black leggings. Who frankly I'd like to shag, given half a chance. Or at least more realistically wank over back in my loathsome Clunt-contaminated studio flat, if only the past ten years had not past and passed me by and rendered even such simple pleasures beyond my limited repertoire. Power off. Power on. ANC on. Pairing. You clunting garbage. I should have paid a bit more and got headphones that actually worked. Zombie hunting. There's one that lurks outside, sneakily enough. I pray for rain, but given a sunny morning it's always there. A wheeled zombie. With its urbane white beard I'd always assumed it must have been the captain of a merchant vessel in its working life, that is when still alive, this being a sea port of sorts. Power off. Useless clunt. Turns out it was a chiropodist.

These zombies still have the capacity to surprise, hence the importance of remaining alert at all times. Exchange of the usual empty, meaningless banalities. Power off. Power on. ANC on. You useless fucking piece of junk. 11.30 am ongoing moderate noise. 12.25 loud TV noise. 14.20 ongoing loud noise. 16.50 ongoing booming voices and music on TV. 17.55 silence. 18.35 TV on loud again. 21.25 very loud voices on TV, cacophony of noise, ongoing. 23.00 TV off. 23.05 - 23.08 chanting. Power off. Clunt. 3.20 am TV on again, loud. Roaming the toxic corridors, zombie hunting. Already taken out the Chief Clunt, the Zombie Chieftain, the Noise Machine. Bits of zombie splattered all over its noisome lair. Zombie parts festooning the shattered TV. The incoherent Irishman now in pieces, soaked in Guinness and vodka. Its more coherent doubled up pal now literally doubled, at least. The sea captain set sail upon his final voyage, departing forever the shores of zombiedom, in several discrete sections. Power off. The dining hall, main refuge for the zombie hordes, now a mausoleum, dissecting room, abattoir. Shining a bright, dark, thick red. Someone once said that old age isn't a battle, it's a massacre. Something to that effect. It's worse than that. It's a zombie parade conducted at deafening volume, from which there is no escape. It's insufferable, literally (Have I used that word before? Yes? Overused? No matter. It's the suffer within that makes it to the nth. degree the *mot juste*). It's an open prison with 24-hour sound effects. It's the scariest thing you could possibly imagine. It's purgatory. It's hell on wheels. Try it sometime. I dare you.

When Evening Falls

I was a teacher at a high school in Birmingham in an earlier incarnation, before a short-lived relationship with a sixth-form pupil ended my career and marriage. After a few months in a squalid bedsit, heavy drinking became alcoholism, resulting in missed appointments, warnings, sanctions. When I got the eviction notice I was two months overdue with the rent. The worst thing of course is not seeing my kids, and not knowing when - or if - I'll see them again. Charlotte and Emily, after the Brontë sisters. Beautiful kids, born just a year apart, now eight and nine years old.

At night I walk around as long as my legs will carry me, keeping clear of noisy groups or anyone who looks at all threatening. Try unsuccessfully to keep warm. But most of all stay alert. And if possible find somewhere hidden or remote where there's the least chance of anyone randomly coming across you. Of course that brings its own dangers when there's nobody around to help if things turn ugly. But as people generally don't want to get involved if something kicks off, making myself inconspicuous seems more of a plus than a minus.

So I try to sleep or rest during the day, lying down as much as possible, then stay awake and alert at night.

Especially between midnight and 4am. The most dangerous time, the witching hours. When from clubs and bars swarm groups of rowdy drunks looking for trouble and amusement. And what could be more amusing to louts high on drugs, alcohol and their own egos than some defenceless individual attempting to find shelter from the pitiless night in a doorway or on the pavement.

Because there's no such thing as community any more - not in this cold and callous world, this post-Thatcher dog-eat-dog anti-paradise. Thinking, I'd happily piss on that creature's grave, that evil piece of shite, given the opportunity. Thinking of the piss soaking into the ground, trickling down into its skull. Happiest day of my life when the Grantham demon was finally exorcized, sent hurtling post-haste to Hell, where it surely belongs.

I remained in Birmingham for the first few weeks of my newly dispossessed existence. Nothing can prepare you for that first night. It overthrows everything you've ever known. Civilization as you've known it vanishes. Everyone you meet is a potential aggressor, with you as potential victim. The very air feels raw and unfriendly in a way you've never experienced before. You're an animal without a home, wary and fearful. Not to mention cold and uncomfortable. And bored. Together with the cold, hunger and fear, boredom is your biggest enemy. Hour upon hour, day after day of discomfort and boredom with nothing to do, read, watch, play.

After a couple of days of this dislocating existence, spent totally alone, I became friendly with a small, skinny guy in his twenties. He'd been living rough for the past few months after leaving prison following a violent attack on his girlfriend - or a falling out, as he put it. He was sleeping nearby in a tiny tent with his dog Rocky, a docile animal, lying alongside. We'd only exchanged a few words, grinning his broken smile, and then I was Marky. Oi Marky, how you doin'.

We spent most of the next couple of weeks palled up. Kyle was cheerful, despite his situation, a jauntiness fuelled largely, it appeared, by an abiding hatred of women. 'Lazy fucking horrible bitches. That's all they are, Marky,' drawing on a spliff, then letting the smoke trickle slowly out the side of his mouth while he gently stroked Rocky's head, playing with its ears, to the animal's obvious delight. 'Fucking hoes on heat. They'll wind you up and wind you in with - y'know - promises of this, that and whatever, and it's all a pack of fucking lies. And then out of nowhere they'll block you, ghost you. Make accusations. The only way to treat a woman - the only fucking right way' (eyes gleaming with hostility) 'is ride the bitch hard, show her who's boss right from the start. Slap the shit out of her if she gets cheeky or steps out of line. If some bitch wants to be with me she does what I fucking say, she's my property. And she better learn that quick smart, or else she'll be getting a smack. I ain't kidding.' The hatred was real and deep and festering.

For some reason he'd taken a shine to me. 'Marky. Oi Marky, look what I got.' A twisted grin, several missing teeth. He'd go thieving, for food, or things he could sell or barter, mainly for drugs, then share the proceeds with me. Might even have been fifty-fifty. 'Ere y'are Marky, have some of that.' He knew I was new to the streets - maybe it was just pity. Whatever the reason he saw me as his mate. Doubtless at least partly due to a feeling of fraternity - the brotherhood of innocent victims of those filthy fucking hoes.

And in those first days and weeks on the street I was glad to have companionship. Everything had been overturned, turned upside down and inside out, so in that context Kyle didn't seem so bad. He'd steal booze, sealed half bottles of whisky, vodka, brandy that I'd knock the neck off, then drink from a plastic cup. Knowing I'd get the shakes without it. He had some secret system for getting stuff out of shops without setting off the security alarms. And I wasn't the only one of our small group he helped. Mandy, a woman in her fifties, on crutches after a bad fall, gaunt and bedraggled, was often on the receiving end of his generosity. She preferred taking her chances on the streets after several frightening experiences in a night shelter, rife with substance abuse and an ever-present threat of violence. Kyle would go out of his way to help her, bring her food, give her money. Bring his dog over for her to pet and cuddle.

The final straw came when he told me of the time he'd half-strangled his then girlfriend. She'd blacked out, then after a few minutes come to, not knowing where she was or what had happened. All because she'd told him she was planning to go out for a few hours and meet some friends and go clubbing. 'Standing there bold as fucking brass, dressed up and painted like a tart, the dirty fucking hoe.' So in a jealous rage he'd almost killed her. That was it as far as I was concerned. I still had a small, hidden emergency fund. Using part of this I bought a one-way ticket to Euston. Early next morning, Kyle still asleep inside his tent, I gathered my stuff - not much more than a backpack, a thin waterproof coat I could shelter under, and a cheap, light, roll-up mattress - and quietly made my escape as Rocky raised his head slowly and watched me with detached curiosity till I was round the corner and out of sight.

The girl was eighteen but looked fifteen or sixteen. Long brown hair, full rosy cheeks. Exceptionally pretty. A luscious youthfulness, primed for sexual adventure. Who could resist her entreaties. Who could not. Me, apparently, for one. For it was 'Lucinda' who led the relationship from the start - it was she who made no secret of what she wanted, and was always the one driving events. She'd stayed back to help after class one day, and everything had escalated swiftly from there. Clandestine meetings at the family home when my wife and kids were out, woodland walks, hand in hand, feeling we'd be less likely to be spotted there than together on the street. In the end my wife found emails between us, hundreds of them - around six hundred in total, I believe, including, embarrassingly, some nude photos. She told the school and I was suspended. Later to be struck off and told I would not be entitled to reapply to teach again.

I was in my late teens when I first read Orwell. I had all his books, yellowing paperbacks with pages falling out that I'd picked up second-hand and read and reread. Among them the books in which he'd documented his social experiments in homelessness. *Down and Out in Paris and London*, parts of *A Clergyman's Daughter* and *The Road to Wigan Pier*. These stories of life on the edges of society in the 1930s fascinated me. Years earlier in the school library I'd come across W.H. Davis's account of living rough and riding freight trains in turn of the century America. Romantic tales for a wide-eyed twelve year-old of battles with hostile train brakemen, camp fires in the wilderness, begging, occasional periods of work, spells in prison. A strange seductive world peopled by mavericks with evocative names like New Haven Baldy, Chicago Slim, Australian Red, the Saginaw Kid, Oklahoma Sam. Much later I read Jack London's *The People of the Abyss*, chronicling his investigations into the East End, clearly directly prefiguring Orwell's expeditions into the same subworld of poverty and homelessness. Little knowing or imagining that decades later in a very different Britain I'd be in the same situation, involuntarily.

Living on the streets in England in the 21st. century sometimes feels like a never-ending exercise in dealing with and mitigating the constant threat of violence. Orwell never mentions any kind of violence directed towards the homeless by the general public (if anything something of the reverse was true, in a common fear of tramps). Of course there were fewer young men around after WW1 - almost a million killed in action, twice that number left with some level of disability, which might have had something to do with it.

This morning I managed to snatch a couple of hours uncomfortable sleep lying on my side in a shop entrance - I hadn't been able to find anywhere safer or more discreet in the early morning and was too tired to walk any further - with my hip bone feeling like it was about to break out of my body. So I was sitting up - it was around seven in the morning - not thinking of anything much except that I needed to get up soon before someone arrived to open the shop. A tall, youngish professional-looking man walking by happened to glance down and saw the empty Costa cup at my feet, and made a remark to the effect that I couldn't be that hard up if I could afford to buy coffee from Costa. I couldn't help noticing how shiny his shoes were, in contrast with my own. I looked up, challenging him with my eyes. He stopped, though I don't think he'd been planning to - it was just a malicious barb in passing, utterly gratuitous. Normally I go out of my way to avoid confrontation, but this morning I just happened to be feeling particularly cold, uncomfortable, miserable and abrasive. 'For your information, pal,' I said, 'I never buy coffee from Costa. If I'm desperate and I've got a pound on me I might get a cup of tea at McDonalds. But this,' picking up the container, which had a pound coin and a few pence in it, 'I got out of a rubbish bin where someone had thrown it.' He said nothing, continuing to look down at me with an unchanged, almost blank expression, any feelings hidden. A few people had stopped to observe the interaction, no doubt hoping something would kick off. 'Anyway,' I continued, 'good attempt to put someone down who's got nothing.' A few murmurs of support from the onlookers. The man began to walk away. 'Nice try,' I shouted pointlessly after him. 'You carry on to your nice warm office. And don't forget to get yourself a filtered decaf caffe latte on the way. Have a great day.' Of course I was running the risk of a kicking, but sometimes you can't help yourself. Almost everyone seems to think you're on the sponge. Even when you look as rough as I do now - I've neither shaved nor had a bath in months.

Occasionally outreach workers come around asking intrusive and impertinent questions. The only thing I want from do-gooders is to be pointed in the direction of a free meal. Anything else, however well-meant (usually involving temporary accommodation), they can keep to themselves - my brief experience of life in a hostel echoed Mandy's, worse even than being on the streets. As for these people, they always come to disturb you just when you've dozed off, peering at you like you're a goldfish in a bowl.

'Hello? Hello? Oh hi. How are you doing? I'm Vicki. I'm an outreach worker for _____. How are you doing this morning?'

'Attempting to sleep.'

'Oh I'm sorry, I didn't mean to disturb you. I was just - '

'Tell you what. I won't come around to where you live asking questions and poking my nose into your life, if you would care to extend the same courtesy to me.'

'We're only trying to see if there's any way in which - '

'There isn't. Goodnight.'

'Well, okay, but don't forget, we're always here if you need us any time.'

'Fine. You know what, I've got my life and you've got yours. Let's just leave it at that.'

I put my arm over my face, and with that I assume she disappeared. Certainly when I next lifted my head she'd gone.

I know I should be more patient - these bleeding hearts are doubtless well-intentioned, and of course they do some good. But for some reason they really rub me up the wrong way. When I think that two years ago I was teaching maths in a high school, and now I'm being patronised and talked down to (literally) by people whose IQ is probably 30 or 40 points lower than mine - on a good day, at least - though I can't help thinking that the last year or so, and especially the past few months, has seriously eroded my mental faculties.

Black mamba and spice are the drugs of choice on the streets. They can be picked up pretty much anywhere, and they're relatively cheap. Kyle was into mamba big time. It's far more powerful than most recreational drugs and its effects far more severe. A single draw on a joint can leave you incapacitated, not knowing where you are or what you're doing, hence 'zombie drug'. It never seemed to affect Kyle adversely, except for a near perpetual craving for it. I've never tried it, or any drugs for that matter - alcohol creates problems enough for me without adding to them. But it's not hard to see why people do this stuff as a way of blotting out reality and getting through the countless hours of boredom. Those who use it say mamba is the cheapest way of knocking yourself out for the day.

Shouting and screaming from somewhere at around quarter past two this morning. Male and female voices. I wasn't asleep, but after that was on high alert. Orwell speaks of the extreme gentleness of the English civilization as he observed it in the 1930s. Does any remnant of that feeling remain? Difficult to believe, living on the streets. No doubt there are many reasons for the change in character of English society, including demographics - and not least the poisonous influence of the Grantham demon. Does England still feel like nowhere else when you come back from abroad - more tolerant, low key, gentle even? Difficult for me to say - I don't travel much these days except from hidden lane to underpass to shop doorway.

I've been sleeping in an underpass the past few nights, in company with maybe a dozen or so other people. It's warmer than many locations, and as the nights begin to draw in there's a real rawness to the air, though winter is still some way off. A couple of nights ago two men had a verbal set-to. Michael, tall, white-bearded, frail, managing to propel himself in a series of strange, jerky movements with the aid of a stick, had been shouting his head off at some imaginary foe. To be confronted by Craig, who'd been trying to sleep, a small, rotund, bespectacled man with a strange high-pitched voice, possibly with something of an Irish lilt, and a peculiar nasal twang. Their bileful exchange, echoing along the tunnel for several minutes, while unpleasant, at least provided a brief interlude in the ocean of boredom.

'Look at you, look at the way you live, no socks on your feet. You're disgusting.'

'Fuck off, you fat bastard. I'm not doing anything wrong.'

'Ah look at you. Your clothes are filthy, you've no self-respect. Shouting your head off, disturbing everybody.'

'Arsehole! Fuck off!'

'Don't you talk to me like that! Don't you *ever* talk to me like that!'

'Fuck off!'

'The police are coming for you. I've notified the police. They'll be here in a few minutes. They'll deal with you.'

'You fat bastard, you don't know what you're talking about. Now fuck off!'

'Don't you talk to me like that! Don't you *ever* - '

'Fuck off!'

'Look at you. Look at the state of you. What a way to live your life. You ought to be ashamed of yourself. Where's your self-respect.'

'Shut the fuck up, you fat bastard. I've done nothing wrong. Fuck off!'

'Don't you talk to me like that! Don't you *ever* talk to me like that! Shouting your head off at all hours, disturbing everybody. The police'll deal with you.'

'Fuck off! Leave me alone, you fat bastard.'

And so on.

Last night, or rather early this morning, I had an encounter such as you learn to expect and fear living on the streets. It's true I've perhaps let my guard down the past few days, become complacent, what with the relative warmth of the underpass and a number of similarly situated people close by. Or maybe it was just cumulative tiredness. Whatever, I'd begun settling down to sleep through the early hours when normally I'd take care to stay awake and alert. The first thing I was aware of was a sudden pain in my back (I was lying face to the wall) which I remember seemed unrelated to whatever it was I was dreaming about. Another sharp pain, this time to my shoulder, maybe aimed at my head - my jacket hood was pulled up, with a thin waterproof coat over my top half, including my head, to block out the light. Now I was at least half awake, though still bewildered - I gathered I was under attack from someone or something. I raised my head and half turned over to see who'd delivered the blows, only to receive another kick, this time to the ear, which half stunned me - the force of the blow cracked my head against the wall.

That finally woke me up. I scrambled to my feet, dodging another kick, one hand held to my ear from the pain, and took in my assailant. A burly sandy-haired yuppie (or so I took him to be), red-faced from his exertions and excitement. Small, unfocused eyes, malevolent, gleeful expression. Out on a drug and/or drink-fuelled jag with the two grinning dolts standing just behind him, a little one-sided violence to round off the evening. By this time the commotion had roused many of the folk around me, and several had risen to their feet as if to give assistance.

All the hours, days, weeks, months of living on the streets of necessity makes you a harder, harsher person. I still felt some fear, but mainly a cold anger and hatred. I suddenly remembered the small canister in my jacket pocket, felt for it, and drew it out with my thumb over the button. A few years ago my wife, after a frightening incident in an otherwise deserted street, had bought online a twin-pack of pepper spray, not realising that possession was illegal in the UK. She'd replaced them with legal defensive sprays. For no particular reason, just before I left the family home forever I'd picked up one of the discarded sprays and put it in my jacket pocket.

I'd never used it, and it was well past its expiry date. But when I pressed the button with my arm outstretched, a stream of greeny/yellowy material shot out, straight into the eyes and mouth of the yuppie. He gave a muffled, choking scream and doubled over. For good measure I administered a similar dose to his friend standing nearby, who reacted in similar fashion - the third lout had already begun running off. I admit that anger got the better of me at this point. Instead of making my escape, which would have been the sensible thing to do, I stepped forward, put one leg behind the legs of my assailant, and gave him a mighty shove. He flew backwards, his head contacting first the wall, then the concrete floor with a satisfying thud. Then repeated the manoeuvre with his friend. Both lay inert bar a few retching moans as one or two of my fellow homeless began laying into them as they lay helpless on the ground.

In stepping forward I'd unwittingly inhaled invisible remnants of the spray still floating in the air. The effect was unpleasant, a palpable discomfort in my throat. I quickly rolled up my mattress, grabbed my bag and headed out into the open air, taking in some water to help my throat once I was safely clear, leaving the two yuppies to their fate. I threw the pepper spray into the river to avoid incriminating myself in case I was picked up. Next day I checked the local papers, but there was nothing, so I guessed that they must have survived. I won't go back there for a while, but will probably do so again at some point as it's one of the warmer places to kip down.

I found a copy of The Big Issue in a bin yesterday morning. I've been reading it on and off ever since. There's an article on the underlying factors in homelessness, appropriately enough, taking information from Crisis and Shelter. The gist of it being that around a quarter of a million people (and rising) are currently experiencing the worst forms of homelessness across England, Scotland and Wales - rough sleeping, sleeping in vans and sheds, stuck in hostels or B&Bs. The cost of living crisis, rising rents, the withdrawal of emergency measures in place during the pandemic all factors. And at the heart of it a lack of affordable social housing, pushing millions of people into insecure, expensive private renting. Over a million households waiting for a decent social home, thousands of homeless children growing up in temporary accommodation. A huge gap between new build social rent homes and those lost through sales and demolitions (a total net loss of 165,000 social homes in the last ten years; demolitions of social housing stock in England in the period 1997-98 to 2021-22 amounting to 231,000). Around 55,000 social rented homes lost and not replaced in England through Right to Buy since 2012 - enough to house nearly every family with children stuck in B&Bs and other temporary accommodation. Though of course there's also the little matter of the UK population rising by around 3.5 million during the period 2012-2021 (and a similar increase in the preceding ten year period).

Right to Buy - yet another exercise in asset-stripping by the Grantham demon. Decent homes that the state had built for people of limited means sold off at a fraction of their market value. Housing lost forever to the nation's social housing stock, not to mention the loss of rental income (rents for remaining council house tenants tended to rise steeply thereafter). A fair proportion of which no doubt later found their way into the hands of money-grabbing landlords. The demon's spiv society in a nutshell.

One of the most striking phenomena of living on the streets for an extended period of time is, in my case at least, a total loss of sexual desire. Orwell talks of 'sexual starvation' among tramps. My experience is quite the opposite - that deprivation appears to have driven out desire. Which perversely is a blessed relief and release from the straitjacket of sexual craving. A distant memory now, those abandoned, intoxicating romps with Lucinda - so distant as to defy belief that they ever actually happened. Just two short years ago. No doubt she's at university now having the time of her life, more achingly attractive than ever, with a retinue of admirers and a full, varied sex life. Her brief excursion with her maths teacher consigned to oblivion, written out of history, deleted.

I could make more of an effort to keep clean and tidy, I suppose, but it's usually more trouble than I can be bothered with. I feel myself sinking inexorably, like Gordon Comstock, 'down, down into the ghost-kingdom, the shadowy world where shame, effort, decency do not exist'. Certainly my mental state at present is of complete inertia. I feel zero motivation to pull myself out of this pit into which I've fallen. I just get through one day at a time, then one long night. And then another day, and another night. And so it goes on.

I never, ever ask for money. I always used to hate that, someone begging shamelessly, monotonously from every passer-by, and would go out of my way to avoid them. So I just leave the coffee cup beside me if I happen to be sitting on the pavement somewhere, usually reading some free newspaper or any reading matter I happen to come across, anything to help pass the time. I usually make a few pounds if I stay there long enough, which tends to be spent on a bottle of something, as strong as I can afford, my staple diet.

One evening a couple of days ago I decided to forgo the drink (I'd actually managed to 'steal' some assorted leftover alcohol from tables outside a pub, pouring the remnants into an empty plastic bottle I keep for the purpose) and instead bought two large orders of fries from McDonalds and brought them back for me and my new friend Sadie. After the underpass incident I never met up with that group again and ended up living on my own for a while, hiding in remote corners overnight. Lately I've latched onto a group of tent dwellers (when it's not raining), one of whom is Sadie, a big woman in her late forties with heavy, coarse features and unspecified mental problems. That is she says she has them, but I've never asked her what they are.

She never actually shut up long enough to eat the fries. I'd be thinking, for Christ's sake stop talking and eat the bloody chips. I'd finished mine while she'd eaten maybe two or three, holding one in her hand for minutes on end, yakking on constantly about incidents in her past, or former friends who'd betrayed her or pissed her off and been unceremoniously cancelled. I don't know how she maintained her impressive BMI, she never seemed to stop talking long enough to eat anything.

That's not to say I didn't appreciate her company, at least until I got bored of it after several hours at a stretch of stuff I'd probably heard before. It's true she was never that interested in what I had to say and never left a gap in the conversation, if you can call it that, for me to get a word in edgeways, though if I forced my way in she would then stop talking and listen with apparent attention, respond briefly to what I'd said, and then was off again. Despite all this, as I say, I enjoyed her company, and she made me laugh for the first time in a long time. Boyfriends failing to adequately service her, especially orally, was one of her favourite topics. 'It doesn't take that much effort. It's really not asking much, is it.' I agreed it wasn't. 'Fucking useless cunts, the lot of 'em.' Smiling broadly. Her last boyfriend (I never found out with any certainty when or how she'd become homeless) had turned out to be addicted to VR porn and ended up not touching her at all. 'Duracell, that's a woman's best friend. Better than all those fucking useless cunts. Never lets you down, never can't be bothered, and lasts as long as it takes to get the job done.' I laughed and agreed that Duracell was clearly the way forward. Grinning at me triumphantly with her yellow teeth.

She always knew best, and everybody else were always arseholes. By her own admission she shed friends like there was no tomorrow. Not surprising as she'd be friendly with you one day, offhand the next, always easily offended. She seemed to take a shine to me, however, as Kyle had done. Unlike Kyle, she invited me to come and stay with her in her tent, with all that implied. Surprisingly she didn't take offence when I declined. Duracell and the device it powered no doubt continued to be a more than satisfactory substitute, though mercifully I never heard any sound effects, despite sleeping right next door to her.

There's a rumour going round that the council are going to come and clear all the tents away. They're a safety hazard, apparently, or health hazard, or biohazard or something of the kind. They're inappropriate (who defines what is or is not appropriate), have been erected in recreational areas of council-operated parks (nondescript areas of litter-strewn grass that nobody ever uses), cause a problem to the general public (they don't), and generally look untidy thus giving offence and an easy target to people who enjoy exercising power (the real reason).

Incidentally, right next to Sadie on the other side lives a guy who is a hazard only to himself. Middle-aged to elderly, white hair balding, eyes behind thick lenses continually flicking here and there, his head constantly jerking and twitching. He has only one conversational gambit, though less conversation than monologue, directed at nobody in particular and uttered, so far as I could tell, apropos of absolutely nothing. 'Tasty, tasty, very very tasty. I like that, do I not. I do, I certainly do.' Repeated ad infinitum in exactly the same form each time. Sadie would look over at him, openly laughing. 'Silly old fucker, doesn't know which day of the week it is. Do you, darling?' 'Tasty, tasty, very very tasty. I like that, do I not. I do, I certainly do.' 'See, he's in another world, poor old fucker.'

Out and about with Sadie she'll call out to passers-by or customers in shops with comments, usually friendly if inappropriate (that weasel word again). 'Love your hair, darling!' 'Lovely dress, sexy lady!' 'Nice haircut, mate! You're really rockin' it!' Or she'll sing along loudly to whatever song is playing in the supermarket, forever looking for attention, trying to make a connection, always overstepping the line of decorum and discretion.

Often dressed in bizarre combinations of top and voluminous trousers. One of her best stories was about when she was working in a care home, or hospitality, I forget which - her stories are often confused, and one tends to merge into another. Called into the manager's office, accused of shitting all over the toilet, floor and surrounding walls of the ladies room, and leaving it in that horrendous state for someone else to clear up. Completely unacceptable. And it wasn't her. She hadn't done it. Okay so she'd had a shit, but she'd never leave the room like she'd been accused of. Though she did once piss herself mid-shift, and the manager or supervisor hadn't allowed her to go home and change, said it was too near the end of her shift, she could last out till then. This with piss running down her legs.

The rumour turned out to be true. The small encampment that had been causing no harm to anyone has been routed, the tents confiscated and the homeless either dispersed or subjected to the council's wrap-around services, when many had already been processed by the system, sometimes numerous times, and due to their 'multiple issues and complex lifestyles' had almost always ended up back on the streets. I'd been away because it had been tipping down, but I met someone in the street I knew, one of the tent dwellers, who told me what had happened. Seems that, predictably, Sadie had mounted a one-woman defensive operation against this violent intrusion and ended up headbutting one of the police. Blood everywhere, calls for back-up, eventually arrested and taken away. And that was the last I saw or heard of Sadie.

Almost all women living rough are escaping 'domestic abuse and other forms of gender-based violence' (Big Issue), as a major component of their homelessness (I never found out if this was the case with Sadie). Recently I managed to steal a couple of books from the library, *London Labour and the London Poor* (which I'd never read), and a copy of the book by Jack London I used to have. Quite an eye-opener reading of the experience of women in the 1850s through Henry Mayhew's highly detailed reportage, and how closely it corresponded with conditions fifty years later in *The People of the Abyss*. Costermongers, always handy with their fists, giving their gal 'a dreadful swole face and a awful black eye'; men living on the wages of prostitution, giving 'a savage punishment to the wretched woman if those wages of sin are wanting'; through jealousy, even upon 'the suspicion of an offence, the "gals" are sure to be beaten cruelly and savagely by their "chaps"' [boyfriends]; a master talking of the 'dustmen' in his employ: 'They spend most of their money that way [drink], and then starve the poor women, and knock them about at a shocking rate, so that they have the life of dogs, or worse.' And on it goes. Forward in time to Jack London: 'Wife-beating is the masculine prerogative of matrimony. They [the men of the ghetto] wear remarkable boots of brass and iron, and when they have polished off the mother of their children with a black eye or so, they knock her down and proceed to trample her…'

Of course conditions for women are generally better now, at least in some parts of the world, than they were back then. But still there are many men like Kyle, and the statistics are horrifying. 81,100 women and girls murdered in 2021 worldwide (Guardian 23 Nov 2022 from UN statistics). This doesn't include all the women and girls killed in war - wars invariably prosecuted by men. 95 per cent of homicide perpetrators at the global level are male (UN Global study on Homicide 2013). And there's the problem in essence.

I was lucky in a way that we were just out of winter, early April, when I was made homeless. Now after six months on the streets we're well into October and it's getting cold. God knows how I'll get through the winter and the freezing nights. I really need to pick up a sleeping bag somewhere. Maybe even a small tent like Kyle's if there's any chance of getting hold of one. I wonder how he's getting on. Back in prison probably. Or shacked up with some unfortunate woman. I don't know what the future holds. It's enough trying to get through each day without worrying overmuch about the future. I just want to see my kids again at some point. That's really the only thing keeping me going.

The Unexpected Rise of Lord Fukkata

A few years back - goodness, how time passes - those old-time Gods, Zeus, Aphrodite, Apollo and the rest - thought it might be mildly interesting to elevate a mere mortal to quasi-God status, then stand well clear and witness the inevitable chaos. And so, partly as an experiment and partly for amusement purposes, was elevated to the pantheon of Gods (or rather, strictly speaking, demigods - a second division outfit on a clearly lower level to the main chorus) the hapless Lord Fukkata aka Jerry Feccata aka the witless and unwitting fall guy.

Born and raised in the Bronx, of Corsican lineage, his parents ran their own small and unsuccessful mail order business till it finally crawled into a dark corner and expired, unloved and unmourned, courtesy of the banking crisis of 2008. Their suspicion that the Fates had it in for them big time had already been thoroughly confirmed by the arrival of their only son Jerome, whose ill temper, stupidity and startlingly low grades at school were followed with gratuitous inevitability on reaching adulthood by long-term unemployment, own-fault car crash, car crash of a marriage, and - well, you get the picture without me having to draw you a diagram. Concluding with a second and this time fatal own-fault car crash. At which point Zeus and his/her/their pals, casting around for a suitably ill-starred victim/subject for their experiment, knew they had found their man/person.

The idea being that anything that goes awry in the world, from war, plague and pestilence to relatively minor matters - parking fines, for instance, or comical slips on dog dirt, or self-inflicted social embarrassments of the lower order - could plausibly be laid at the door of Lord Fukkata. Thus he would take on to himself - even as Jesus took all our sins unto himself, that we, being dead to sins, should live unto righteousness - responsibility for everything that goes wrong in the world - large and small - so wiping the slate clean for humanity in perpetuity. Hence Lord Fukkata, God of fuck-ups. Not just his own, but everyone's, everywhere, and throughout time (courtesy of a neat retrospective sleight of hand). Harold Godwinson at the Battle of Hastings? Lord Fukkata. Doug Sanders missing a simple putt on the 18th at St Andrews that would have won him the 1970 Open? Lord Fukkata. Your keenly disliked next door neighbour tripping over the power cable while cutting their front lawn and falling headfirst into adjacent rose bushes, thus giving you the first good laugh of a miserable, depressing week? Okay, so you get the point.

That at least was the idea, though it didn't quite work out as intended, despite (or because of) Fukkata's propensity for fuck-ups far outstripping the capacity of most mortals.

And so we find Lord Fukkata lounging on his lounger one day, unshaven as ever, his robe, stained with wine and other more noxious substances, gaping wide, a glaring affront to civilized society pretty much anywhere, but especially the heavenly realms.

'Hey F, so what do you want to do about this ephemeral being - this guy, as you would say? That is if you insist on continuing to interfere with the lives of mortals in direct contravention of official policy.'

The speaker, the highest ranking of Lord Fukkata's officially appointed minions (he/she/they was/were called Mmomoma, for reasons that presently escape me, and whose name understandably defeated Lord F's resentful and half-hearted attempts at correct pronunciation, tending to come out sounding something like 'Momma' or some variant thereof, the effort involved adding grist to his mill of perpetual irritation), was a gender-fluid entity with a studiously androgynous appearance that in combination with a provocatively light and airy mode of speech and dry, official manner irritated the holy bejasus out of the unsophisticate formerly known as Jerry Feccata.

'This guy? Who's *this guy*? What's with you people and all the dumb questions? And that's Lord F to you, Momma Mia! And bring me some coffee, will you?'

(What the above speech actually sounded like phonetically was, 'Dis guy? Who's *dis guy*? What's wid you numb nuts an' all the fuckin' questions? An' dat's Lord F to you, ya dumb cluck. An' bring me some cawfee, willya?')

'We're out of coffee.'

'What do you mean we're out of coffee?'

'We're out of coffee.'

'Out of coffee? What the Bruce Springsteen do you dumb clucks do all day? You want me to drink water? Just get me some coffee.'

'Maybe we got wine. I mean I think we've got wine if you'd prefer that?'

'Jesus H Christ! I ask for something as simple as a cup of coffee and it turns into some kind of production number! Just get the fucking coffee!'

Just as this discussion was developing nicely it was interrupted by the sudden appearance of a gender-fluid herald from the upper pantheon with a unique approach to the announcement of his/her/their mistress.

'Rrup!! Jinga!! Rrrrrr!!! Jinga!! Jinga!! Ching, ching, ching!! Bd-up, bd-up, bd-up!! Rrup!! Rrup!! Bdum, bdum, bdum!! Wwaah!! Wwaah!! Rrrrrr!!!' And so on, followed by, 'Nothing! I repeat - Nothing! I emphasise - Nothing! I reiterate - Nothing! I encapsulate - Nothing! I - '

'Get on with it!' (voice off)

' - would give me more pleasure than to - '

' - this ridiculous nonsense every single time - '

' - the presence of my Heavenly mistress Aphrodite, of sweet delight and love and graciousness - '

' - trying my patience - '

' - daughter (so to speak) of Ouranos, sister (in a manner of speaking) of the Gigantes, the Meliae, and the Furies, called Alekto, Tisiphone and Megaira - '

'Okay, that's enough. Scram!'

And as the herald vanished there appeared without further ado the great Goddess Aphrodite. She'd been meaning to pop down for some time, partly to get to know their new recruit a little better, and partly to offer a word of advice/warning, but this was her first time of actually seeing Lord Fukkata in the flesh (of which rather too much was on display), and she was immediately intrigued. Unlike literally everybody else who'd ever met or even just seen him in passing, whether on Earth or in the heavenly realms, far from being repelled and/or disgusted, she found herself immediately attracted, and enchanted especially by his complete indifference to her charms, a characteristic which had all the heady appeal of novelty. He looked to her startlingly bright (through excitement) in fact near-fluorescent eyes uncannily like the overweight, out-of-condition double of Randall 'Tex' Cobb, former professional boxer, martial artist and actor, a rough and ready tough guy who'd taken on and beaten the likes of Earnie Shaver and Leon Spinks. He greeted her with a Grade A unfriendly expression, glowering suspiciously behind his heavy, drooping moustache. She smiled encouragingly.

'Don't you just love these genderqueers? They come over here taking our jobs and our - oh no, wait, that's something else entirely!'

Unlike the usual rather vapid and passive depictions of her through the ages - she felt Botticelli had a lot to answer for on that score - Aphrodite in reality cut an impressively dynamic all-action figure, combined with a temperament which demonstrated an irresistible urge to express strong opinions on pretty much everything. Yes, she was replete with sensuous lips and dreamy eyes (as prescribed), but she also had a strictly non-ethereal pair of sturdy thighs, her ankles were not the least bit shapely, and she possessed an upper torso that suggested of serious bodybuilding in her spare time, in fact suggested that Sugar Ray Leonard would have had his hands full over twelve rounds.

'So, how do you like it here?'

'Like?'

'Yes, like. Do you like it here?'

'Here?'

'Here, in the lower pantheon.'

'Is that what you people call this place?'

'I'm not 'you people'. I am Aphrodite. And yes, it's known as the lower pantheon, to distinguish it from the upper pantheon. So, to return to my question, and before I get completely bored of asking it, how do you like it here?'

'You mean in the lower pantheon?'

'Yes.'

'You mean how do I like it here?'

'Yes, that's right.'

'So, just to clarify, you're asking me how I like it in the lower pantheon?'

'Correct.'

'Well, truth is I hadn't that much of an alternative to this whole deal - that is apart from spending the rest of my life being dead.'

Aphrodite laughed loudly.

'You're very funny!'

Lord F scowled.

'Anyway, surely it's not that bad?'

'No, it's not that bad, except I can never get any goddam thing to drink. And I got this dumbass chief assistant called Momma, or something like that, who's about as much use as a chocolate dick.'

'Yes, I've heard he's a bit of a prick. Not unlike my herald Dwoobus. In fact I hear they hang around together a fair bit, if you know what I mean, when they're off-duty.'

'No.'

'Oh yes, apparently.'

'So what?'

'That's all. So everything's going okay?'

'Okay?'

'Yes, I mean is everything going as well as can be expected?'

'What, down here in the lower precinct?'

'Pantheon.'

'Same thing.'

'So what's the answer?'

'You mean as to whether everything's going as well as can be expected?'

'Yes.'

'Yes.'

'No complaints?'

'Complaints?'

'Yes, complaints, problems, difficulties.'

'None that I can - '

'So everything's fine?'
'Fine?'

And so, improbably (to state it mildly), it was love at first sight. On Aphrodite's side, that is, as Lord F continued to show next to no sign of interest, which only served to increase the sense on Aphrodite's part that this hulking, uncommunicative, unshaven caveman of a demigod was the camembert to her cream cracker. Yet there remained one test to perform, her standard method of appraisal, his reaction to which would reveal all as to a possible future together.

Thus she began to express the view, calmly yet forcibly, that all this transgender/gender-fluid he/she/they/xe/xem/xyr floating sense of masculine/feminine stuff was a big steaming bunch of baloney, that there were men, and then on the other hand there were women, and apart from a few somewhat ambiguous exceptions to prove the rule (not including the Gods and demigods of the upper and lower pantheons) that was your lot, the only credible options on the table, whereas how you choose to behave in terms of how you view and present yourself along the whole spectrum of masculine/feminine is entirely your choice, and has nothing - nothing (she repeated), to do with gender, that the problem at the heart of this issue being the correlation of 'masculine' and 'feminine' behaviours with gender - with being male or female, that gender-fluid should read behaviour-fluid, regardless of gender (but it wouldn't be as much fun then), otherwise you're back in the bad old days of glaring gender stereotypes, all pure regression, the playing of self-indulgent semantic games, and harmful because it entrenches archaic and limiting stereotypes, that the whole spectrum of behaviour is available to everyone, regardless of whether you're a man or woman, that to equate behaviour with gender is to get the whole issue arse about face and set society back minimally fifty years, that what's wrong with the whole concept can be neatly summed up in two words - gender identity, that certainly in her own case her gender had nothing to do with how she thought, felt, behaved or self-identified (though she conceded the matter was complicated by that fact she was a God and in fact with Zeus pretty much CEO of the whole pantheon of Gods).

These so-called gender queers! It was all me, me, me! Look at how different and interesting I am with all these absurd labels I've stuck on myself, when in fact you're probably really not, but at least in your own mind you're the absolute centre of the universe due to how unusually interesting you've become since you stuck one or more of at least fifty available meaningless labels on yourself and become a magnet for controversy, when in fact the reality is that the vast majority of people couldn't give even the faintest shadow of a fuck about any of it, as everyone's seen or done it all before over many, many decades, and we're not surprised, shocked or even mildly interested, but only incredibly bored, and so she continued for quite a while.

Precisely what Lord F was thinking the while - or rather precisely what he would have thought about this thesis had he the capacity to do so, is anybody's guess.

'Have you done?' he said when at last she relapsed into an expectant silence.

'Yeah. What do you think?'

'I need a drink. A big one. Or two.'

He called to Momma Mia.

'Get me a whiskey, will you.'

'We're out of whiskey.'

'You don't agree?'

'About what?'

'What we were just discussing.'

'I didn't know we were discussing anything. I thought you were making a speech.'

She began to laugh. She laughed and laughed, and the echo of her laughter echoed within the marble halls for almost as long as the speech itself.

'Oh deary me! That's a good one! Well, you'll be pleased to know you've passed my test with flying colours!'

'What test?'

'The test of my own invention, specifically designed to measure interest in abstract reasoning. And I'm delighted to be able to report that you showed no response whatsoever!'

'You mean you don't actually believe all that stuff you were saying?'

'Whether I believe it or not is beside the point. For the purpose of the experiment I proposed a line of argument, and then pursued it as far as logic dictated. I may or on the other hand I may not believe it. But the vitally important thing is that you weren't the least bit interested!'

Lord Fukkata looked genuinely confused.

'Why's it important?'

'Why? You ask me why?' She frowned. She was so used to adulation. 'Isn't it obvious?'

'No.'

She relaxed and smiled.

'Well, I'm sure all will become clear, even to you, in due course. However, in the meantime, there is something I need to tell you.'

'What?'

'Well, not to beat around the bush, the Gods of the upper pantheon are becoming quite concerned about your activities, specifically your interference in the affairs of the ephemeral beings, though I less so.'

'You less so what?'

'Just I less so.'

'Hey, Momma Mia, get me some wine, will you?'

'We're out of wine.'

'You know you cannot continue to interfere in the lives of mortals.'

'What do you mean we're out of wine?

'We're out of wine.'

'I thought you said we were out of coffee.'

'Are you listening to me? I tell you this is of great import if you are not to feel the wrath of the Gods, and of my father Zeus in particular.'

(She generally qualified the precise nature of her daughterhood with, 'Well, sort of. Maybe. It's complicated.')

'We're out of wine and coffee. And whiskey.'

'Just get me the fucking wine, will you. Jesus.'

'Do not provoke my anger!' She managed to force a smile, albeit a threatening smile. 'It is never wise to provoke the anger of the Gods.'

Lord Fukkata looked up at Aphrodite briefly with a disinterested, sullen expression, before looking around for Mmomoma, who'd vanished. He wondered if the annoying minion would actually produce something for him to drink this time, or if he, Lord F, would be forced to apply his boot to Momma's ethereal gender-fluid ass.

'Now listen. You must stop interfering. It's just not the way we do things any more. Do you understand? Do you promise to do that for me?'

'Sure,' said Lord F, who had no intention of doing anything of the sort, given the enjoyment he derived in exercising his powers of malicious intervention.

'Very well. Then we shall say no more about it. And now I shall leave you for the present. But not, I hope, for long.'

She smiled expressively, took a last, surreptitious look at the rolls of fat around his midriff and the ominous bulge in his stained boxers, then with a gentle sigh departed for the upper pantheon.

Lord F had always been determined (if that's the right word for a past master of apathy) to push things along a bit and up the averages. Manipulating the score line, as his critics (of which there were many) might have said. But his reasoning (if one can so describe the muddy convolutions that passed for his thought processes) was that if fuck-ups were his business, then the more the merrier and the bigger the better.

'She's right, you know.'

'Who's right?'

Who do you think, you dumb cluck.

'The Goddess Aphrodite, my Lord F. Let us review the evidence of the past week.'

To Lord Fukkata's surprise (perhaps not fully appreciating the momentary fluidity of the masculine/feminine dynamic) Mmomoma's voice had abruptly dropped by the best part of an octave since he/she/they had spoken just a moment ago, to become a commanding baritone, and at the same time he/she/they had puffed out his/her/their chest and thrust forward ditto chin, thus adopting an unequivocally masculine posture.

'Take last Tuesday, for example - '

'What's happened to your voice?'

'Nothing. I - '

'Fine. Then get me a beer, will you.'

'We're out of beer. Now, last Tuesday - '

'Hey!'

'Speaking of last Tuesday' (Lord F sunk down morosely in his lounger and thought dark thoughts, many of which centred around a number of interesting fates which he thought should befall Momma Mia, if there was any justice in the universe - which clearly there wasn't), 'there occurred the incident of the inkpot. An inoffensive elderly clerk working away at his writing desk copying by guttering candlelight some long and intricate document - no doubt laborious work at the best of times. At which point you deliberately upset his inkpot, filled full with ink, all over the document, resulting in his immediate dismissal and probable destitution.'

'It's just great being able to go back in time and fuck people up! There's no limit to what you can do. Or what *I* can do.'

Mmomoma gave him a disdainful look.

'Or take the case of the dancing competition, where once again you intervened to negative effect. The clear favourites, a talented and charming young couple, performing the routine of their lives. And you just had to ensure that the woman's sequinned gown became entangled in her heels, causing her to slip suddenly sideways, get elbowed in the face by her partner, fall through the scenery, then collapse offstage in a tearful heap with mild concussion and torn ligaments in her ankle.'

'That was something, wasn't it! I just can't get enough of this stuff!'

'And these are just among the more spectacular of your interventions. That was on Wednesday. What happened on Thursday? That poor elderly couple. The gentleman bringing his infirm bedbound wife a nice pot of tea, and promptly tipping the contents all over her, badly scolding her arms. I believe she spent some time in hospital. And all courtesy of my Lord Fukkata.'

'Hahaha! Classic! You better be making a record of all these hilarious incidents, Momma Mia. I wish I had them on video.'

'I am not.'

'Well, get on it. Just remember you're here to do what I tell you. With no back chat. Now get me something to drink, and make it snappy.'

Despite Aphrodite and Mmomoma's advice and admonition, Lord F failed by an enormous margin to mend his ways, resulting in a curt summons to attend Zeus at his pleasure in the upper pantheon. The summons, and the tone of it, managed to discomfort even Lord Fukkata.

He read it over several times, breathing (snorting) heavily the while in consternation. Finally he looked up, and seeing his chief minion close by, held out the sheet of papyrus.

'What do you make of this?'

'I don't know. I can't read it when you thrust it in my face.'

'Take it, then.'

Mmomoma took the document and read it while Lord Fukkata sat gloomily staring ahead at nothing.

'It appears that you are summoned to the upper pantheon at the pleasure of the great Lord Zeus.'

'I know that. I can read. What I mean is, what's the meaning behind it? Why am I being summoned? And in such a way.'

The summons was peremptory, and the words interfere, meddle, and fiasco figured prominently. Mmomoma thought the reason for the directive was blindingly obvious, but held his counsel.

'I want you to go up there and find out what this is all about. Now. Straight away. Do whatever it takes to find out the facts. And I mean the details.'

'Who me?'

'Yes, you. Now get on with it!'

Mmomoma, dressed in his newest and whitest robes, slowly and reluctantly made his way to the upper pantheon, which was similar to the lower pantheon, but bigger, and with longer, wider, more elaborate staircases, and with considerably more marble.

Zeus's gender-fluid third-ranking herald conveyed Mmomoma's request for an audience, and after a long wait he/she/they was/were ushered into the presence of the (joint) ruler of the Heavens/God of sky and thunder. Mmomoma not a little disconcerted to find that far from the anticipated private interview, sitting before him/her/them was/were practically the full complement of the Gods, among them Apollo (a bargain basement Elvis, strumming his lyre quietly in a corner), Athena (determinedly sharpening the point of a spear), Ares (ex-lover of Aphrodite, assuming fatuously belligerent poses), Dionysus (drunk but only slightly disorderly) etc.

etc. And seated at their head in state were Zeus and Aphrodite (to Mmomoma, Zeus looked somewhat like a young Joe Bugner, only with a long, grey beard - not necessarily a good look).

Lord Fukkata's minion genuflected nervously for several seconds before this impressive array of talent, then rose, waiting to be addressed.

Long moments later Zeus spoke.

'You wished to have conference with me?'

'Yes, my Lord Zeus,' Mmomoma's voice pitched high and with a slight nervous tremor. He/she/they hesitated. 'That is' (oh yes, this is by far the deepest hole I've ever been dropped into), 'I was wondering my Lord - ' (zero thanks to the idiot Lord F for creating this whole ludicrous mess) ' - whether it would be possible to inquire as to - ' (what in the name of Marvin Hagler to say?) ' - that is, as to the reason for summoning my Lord Fukkata to your presence?'

'What!!!'

The Heavens shook, dark clouds gathered swiftly overhead and a low-pitched rumble of thunder could be heard.

'Calm down', said Aphrodite. 'You always overreact.'

'I am not overreacting. Don't always accuse me of overreacting.'

'Well don't overreact, then. Now - it's Mmomoma, isn't it - '

'I shall handle this matter.'

'No, father/father-in-law, I think it would be better if you leave it to me.'

'I said I will handle this.'

'You'll only overreact. Leave it to me.'

'I will not overreact!!!'

'There, you see, you're doing it again. Now, Mmomoma, would you mind returning to your master, and requesting his personal presence here. Tell him it's a matter of pressing importance that requires his prompt attendance. In person.'

Mmomoma, only too glad to escape, bowed low and scuttled away.

'I could have said all that,' grumbled Zeus.

'I know you could, in theory, but in practice you'd have made a meal of it.'

After comprehensively chewing out Mmomoma for failing to return with the full facts, Lord Fukkata stomped his way to the upper echelon and tried to the best of his (severely limited) ability to state his case.

'So what do we do when it's some guy who never puts a foot wrong. Never makes any mistakes. Always bucking the system. Gets away with all kinds of shit. I thought we could just - '

'Look, get this through your thick skull once and for all. We don't intervene any longer - that kind of direct interference just doesn't fly in the modern world. We wait for them to fuck up, and then - '

'We offer them a helping hand?'

A distinct warning rumbling was heard from the direction of the Heavens at what Zeus thought might be (but wasn't entirely sure) an attempt at mockery (deciding in the end that it wasn't, but more likely just outright stupidity).

'How often do I have to explain basic procedure to you? No, we don't offer any kind of a helping hand. We do nothing. They put the fuck-up down to bad luck or Fate or whatever - which, whether they know it or not, takes the form - may Gaia forgive me - of you, Fukkata. Putting them in the clear, all set for their next fuck-up. That's how the system works. Got it now?'

'Yeah,' in a sulky, reluctant voice.

'Thank Christ for small mercies.'

'I just thought it might expedite (he'd heard the word somewhere, been waiting for just the right moment to deploy it and, astonishingly, had managed to use it in the correct context) matters if we helped the process - which you so expertly explained, I might say - ' (Lord F had at least learned to apply the grease amongst all these chancers) ' - along a little bit.'

'What the holy mother of fuck are you talking about?'

'Well, I was just thinking it'd be more credit to you guys upstairs if we increased the volume of fuck-ups worldwide, so that then we could - '

'Don't.'

'What?'

'Try thinking. Time and experience has demonstrated very clearly that you are supremely ill-equipped for the task. Leave the thinking to me and my fellow supreme beings, and just do what you've been told. Dig?'

The sky now boomed with ominous heavy thunder at this minor outburst of Zeus's anger. But in fact it had zero effect on Lord Fukkata, who had never taken much notice of the weather provided he was indoors sprawled in an easy chair in front of the tv with alcohol and snacks to hand. The weather, generally speaking, was something that happened to somebody else, and Jerry Feccata had never troubled himself unduly by anything that happened to anyone else.

'I dig.'

He dug, but that didn't mean he liked it. In fact he deeply resented it. Jerry had never liked being told what to do, and as Lord Fukkata he liked it even less. From early childhood, even when what he liked to do had proved counterproductive (as it always did) he preferred that to the alternatives - such as thinking before he acted, or putting in time and effort to a task, or taking good advice, or learning from his mistakes, and so on.

And in this case he once more stayed true unto himself, ignoring the warning from the highest council of the Gods, and continuing to fuck up himself by fucking up others. Leading to an angry Zeus in a secretly-arranged private interview (in the hope of sidestepping Aphrodite) informing Lord F of his banishment to the Underworld.

'You've fucked up here for the last time, my friend. It's no good, we gave it a shot, but it just didn't work out. So you're going down for a long, long time. Maybe forever. No big deal. I'll put you in touch with our guy in the Underworld, in fact my brother Hades. He's nowhere near as mean or rough as his reputation suggests. You'll like him. And you'll like it there. Just try to stay on his right side, that's all. And no more fuck-ups while you're down there. Dig?'

Lord F muttered something unprintable under his breath. The Heavens rumbled once more.

'Yeah, whatever,' he said reluctantly.

In response, when she (inevitably) heard via roundabout means of her favourite's imminent banishment, and before Zeus's dictate could be executed, Aphrodite (incensed by Zeus's attempt to circumvent her joint authority) played her trump card, declaring her love for Lord Fukkata, and her irrevocable intention to marry him forthwith. To be met with a predictable bellow of rage from Zeus that got everyone's ears ringing. He then proceeded to make a number of unpleasant and personal remarks on the subject of Aphrodite's tangled love life, focusing on the sheer quantity (over quality) of her former lovers. And concluding with the suggestion that this current infatuation was just another of her short-lived adventures, and it was high time she mended her ways and behaved in a fashion that -

'Oh really?' Her voice cut like a winter wind. 'And what about your many, many wives, and even more numerous 'conquests', if that isn't too polite a term? You'd need to hire a Plaxton Panorama double deck on the ubiquitous Volvo tri-axle chassis to accommodate all your former wives and paramours.'

The Heavens shook, but Aphrodite had heard it all before and remained visibly unimpressed.

'Anyway, I care not one whit what you or anybody else says. I'm having him, and that's an end of it! He's not going anywhere near Hades or the Underworld. Not on my watch!'

And so we find, in the fullness of time, Lord F packing his things in preparation for a move to the upper p. Or rather Mmomoma doing the work for him.

'You do know she's been around the block a few times, to put it mildly?' said Mmomoma, sorting through his master's socks and underclothes, holding each item at arm's length.

'Who cares. If it's a choice between that and being banished to the Underworld for the rest of time, it's a no-brainer.'

Which should suit you perfectly, my Lord F.

'By the way, my Lord, I wonder if I could ask you…' Mmomoma hesitated. 'That is…'

'Well?'

'That is - what about me, my Lord?'

'What about you?'

'Well, when you marry the great Goddess Aphrodite and take up your position in the upper pantheon, I assume I'll be out of a job. Not to put too fine a point on it, I'll be redundant.'

An unaccustomed smile edged its way cautiously across Lord F's usually morose features.

'Oh yeah, I hadn't thought of that. That's a shame!'

'My Lord Fukkata, forgive me for omitting to inform you earlier, but I believe we've just received a large consignment of alcoholic beverages of various kinds. Allow me to mix you a refreshing martini.'

The smile on Lord F's face seemed to gather momentum.

'Sure, why not. I guess I deserve it. In fact make it a double! And who knows, maybe I can find a way to take you with me after all.'

'Oh Lord F, that would be simply - '

'I said maybe. We'll just have to see how it goes. Think of yourself as being on probation.'

'I don't know what to say, my Lord. I - '

'Just get me the goddam drink, will you.'

And so off went Mmomoma to fix two martinis, one (double) for Lord Fukkata, and one (secretly and against the rules) for him/her/them self. He/she/they felt that if anyone needed it, it was him/her/them.

Printed in Great Britain
by Amazon